Beautiful Revenge

A Good Wife Novel

SIENNA BLAKE

Beautiful Revenge: a novel / by Sienna Blake. – 1st Ed.
First Digital Edition: September 2017
Published by SB Publishing
Copyright 2017 Sienna Blake

ISBN-13: 978-1974493418
ISBN-10: 1974493415

Cover art & paperback formatting services by Romacdesigns: http://romacdesigns.com.
Cover art copyright 2017 Romacdesigns. All Rights Reserved Sienna Blake. Stock images: shutterstock
Content editing & proofreading services by Book Detailing.
Proofreading services by Proof Positive: http://proofpositivepro.com.

The characters and events portrayed in this book are fictional. Any similarity to real persons, living or dead, is coincidental and not intended by the author.

Introduction

Dear Readers,
As this book is set in England, it is written in British-English (such as 'colour' instead of 'color' and 'realise' instead of 'realize').

Dedicated to all of us imperfect humans who have ever erred.
And to those who love us enough to forgive.

Chapter One

Alena

There is a locked wooden box I hide under my bed. I only dare to take it out when my husband is away.

I stand at the edge of the tall casement window in my bedroom and peer around the curtains, my fingers gently pulling the thick pallid-blue satin aside. Mist hangs across the moors beyond the Worthington Manor grounds, the early morning light making everything seem dusky. Half-real. Like I'm still dreaming.

I'm just in time to see the dark figure of my husband duck into the back seat of his silver Bentley, parked in the gravel driveway below that curls around the towering marble fountain. The uniformed chauffeur shuts his door and marches around to the driver's side. My heart rate climbs steadily as the vehicle purrs down the mile-long carriage driveway, past the lake, and disappears through the cluster of trees that edge this thousand-acre estate.

I force myself to count down five minutes just in case he has forgotten something and decides to return. I made that mistake once.

...three...two...one.

He's gone.

He won't be back for two days this time.

My body trembles with relief as I close my curtains completely, leaving my room lit only by my vintage shell-like bedside lamp.

I don't go to the bed. Not yet.

I tread on soft, thick carpet, across the expanse of my room to my door, painted the same robin's egg blue as my curtains. In fact, this exact weak, placid shade of blue is the only colour accenting my ash wood, marble and cream room, overly decorated with crystal chandeliers, antique furniture and a ridiculous number of fringed pillows.

I turn my doorknob and peer outside into the second-floor hall. Worthington Manor, an early Georgian countryside mansion, has been in my husband's family for over three hundred years, or so I hear him boast at dinners and parties. The marble hallways stretch along in two wings, with dozens of rooms branching off on either side. The high vaulted ceilings and walls are all crammed with intricate cream plasterwork, making me feel like I live inside a wedding cake.

I listen. I hear no one. Not the footmen or maids. Not even Emily.

I close my door again. My bedroom is lockable but only my husband has the key. As far as I'm aware, he either takes it with him when he leaves on business or he hides it somewhere. I've looked for it during his absences, late at night when the rest of the house is asleep. I could never find it.

I run to my unmade bed and fling myself to the lush carpet beside it, another victim to the washed-out blue colour. My fingers shake with greed as I reach underneath, find purchase on the grainy wood and tug it out. The moment my eyes land on the simple mahogany box, a little bigger than an Old Testament Bible, a brass lock on the front, my throat starts to swell from the inside. I can feel the memories pressing up against me, tapping like hungry beggars against glass. I can hear *his* ghost whispering from over my shoulder. Like he's standing right behind me, brushing the hair off my neck, lips tracing my earlobe.

Alena Ivanova...

I stumble to my feet and collapse onto my bed. I pull the box into my lap, my fingers clutching it as if it were a forgotten child. It's an anchor tying me, my past, and my present together.

Until the end of time, Alena...

I draw out the locket at the end of a long silver chain around my neck. I crack it open and pull out the hidden key inside, my fingers slipping slightly as they have now gone clammy. My breathing shakes out through my teeth as I push the key into the rusty lock.

Why do I do this to myself? Every time I open it, it cuts open this old, unhealed wound. But I can't help myself. I can't bear to throw this box away. I can't let go. Perhaps this pain that I force upon myself is my only way to absolution, self-flagellation in the hopes it will one day redeem me from my greatest mistake.

I turn the key with a slight effort and I hear the familiar click. I'm surprised when water drops onto the lid. I'm crying, hot tears leaking like blood from my eyes. I don't wipe them away.

I take a breath and open up my past.

They are all there, each piece I saved, nestled in the red velvet heart. Each jagged memory. I pull out each item one by one. I hold it, caress it, before placing it aside on my bedcover:

a shredded piece of white lace for an innocence left behind,

a broken piece of vinyl for a love song that would never be mine, and finally…

a photo.

A photo of a man with stormy hair and summer's-day eyes.

Chapter Two

Five years ago…

Nothing is as cold as a Russian winter. It's the kind of cold that seeps into your bones, turning your marrow to ice. The kind of cold that stabs at your lungs every time you inhale. That slides under your nails like splinters, turning your fingers blue. I shiver and huddle further into the layers of mismatched blankets that we've scavenged from various places. It's not even winter yet. It's barely November.

God help us when winter really starts.

I feel him shift behind me on our tiny mattress, rusty springs protesting every movement. His arms wrap around me, pulling me back against his hard body. I melt into him. I can barely feel his body heat with the layers of clothes we both wear. When he holds me, the warmth comes from the inside.

I shift around until I am facing him, our breaths making a tiny tropical planet between us. It's my favourite planet, his and mine. The moon is full. It shines straight through the thin, cracked window pane, giving everything in our cramped St Petersburg studio apartment a silvery glow. I gaze at him through my lashes, my breath catching in my lungs. He is the most beautiful man in the whole wide world. Not that I've ever left St Petersburg, but even if I did, I know that no one else could hold a candle to Dimitri Volkov.

He has midnight hair that's long overdue for a haircut. It sits like a thunderstorm, dark and wild around his head, making him look like a kind of devil. He has high chiselled cheekbones, a strong jaw, thick lips sculpted in a cupid's bow. Deep-set eyes that can flash with cobalt fire and brimstone or invite me to drown in them like a secret lagoon. Women look at him all the time when we walk together. His beauty is obvious. But he only ever looks at me. Only me.

He is mine, the only thing that's ever been mine. And I am his.

"Why aren't you sleeping?" he says in Russian, his voice deeper than other nineteen-year-old boys. It's a man's voice. It takes on this gravelly tone when he's telling me off, the one that he has right now. The one I secretly get a thrill out of.

"*Someone* was snoring," I tease, hoping to get a rise out of him.

He lets out a snort. "I was not."

"Like a bear. Holding a chainsaw."

He laughs. I love the sound, deep and rich, rumbling through my chest like approaching thunder, plucking at something inside of me. "You're mixing your metaphors. But when you're a famous writer, everyone will be using them."

I withhold a sigh. "One day, I guess."

He shakes me lightly, staring right into me. "You will. You can do anything, Alena." His tone is firm and dares me to deny his words. He has more confidence in me than I have in myself.

Sometimes it's hard to dream of being a writer. Because wanting it, chasing it, believing it, is like reaching for a star and trying to pluck it from the heavens. Impossible. Here on earth we have real problems, like staying warm and getting enough to eat. As if my stomach hears this thought, it lets out a low growl. I flinch, hoping he hasn't noticed it.

Dimitri frowns at me, telling me he has. "Are you hungry?"

"No," I lie. I wince when my traitorous belly lets out a louder, more insistent growl.

"Didn't you eat the sandwiches I left for you before I went to work?" He works so hard, often pulling double shifts at the factory, but he still finds time to make me food for school.

"Yes," I say, drawing out the word.

Dimitri's mouth curls up, anger already flashing in his eyes. "Did you eat *all* of them?"

I chew my lip, guilt winding up an invisible staircase inside me. "There was a young boy, you see, not even ten. He was all alone on the street. Begging. He looked so hungry and cold and—"

"You gave a sandwich to him," Dimitri says, finishing my sentence. It wasn't even a question.

"I couldn't help it. He seemed so much hungrier than I was…" I swallow back the excuses on my tongue as Dimitri's eyes narrow. I avert my gaze, hoping he doesn't see what I've left unsaid.

"You gave him *all* of your sandwiches?"

I don't answer him. I don't have to. I can never hide from him. He can read the guilty look on my face. He can see everything inside of me.

"Alena," he says, his voice rising in volume, "I know you want to help him, you want to help everyone, but you're not helping yourself."

"I'm fine, Dimi."

"You are not fine," he bellows. "You're starving to death and you're giving away your fucking food." His hands shake by my face as if he's ready to choke me. I don't flinch. Not at all. Dimitri's anger is like a flare, bursting out in a mad rush of colour and noise, lighting up the room. But he would never hurt me. Never. I'm as sure of that as I am that the spring will follow winter.

I touch his cheek with my palm and he softens at my touch. His fingers tangle in my hair as he pulls my head into his chest. He lets out a half-groan, half-sigh against my hair. "What am I going to do with you, little lamb?" His soft lips press against my forehead, and I feel his kiss all the way down to my toes.

"Love me?" I whisper.

He presses me closer. "I already do. So much."

My heart tumbles and spins a glorious dance in my chest. "You worked late," I say, changing the subject. He wasn't home when I buried myself in the bed.

"I had to. I think I'm close, Alena," he says in a hushed tone, his voice vibrating with excitement. "I think I'm really close."

I glance up at him. "Really?"

He nods, his eyes sparkling like sapphires. "The talk is that they're letting go of the junior accounts officer. And they're grooming me to fill in."

I force a smile bigger than I feel to hide my anxiousness. Dimitri isn't just good with his hands, he's good with numbers too. He can add up large sums in his head. He can look at a sheet of numbers and make sense of them. The same way that words speak to me, numbers speak to him. He amazes me with his affinity with them. He's been *really close* to a promotion and a pay raise for months now. I think his boss—the fat, greedy bastard—just dangles these promises over Dimitri's head to get him to take on accounting duties without being paid extra for them. Dimitri never sees it like that. He wants this promotion so badly he's blinded to being used. He's not the only one of us who dreams of something better.

"Dimitri Volkov, Junior Accounts Officer," he says in a reverent tone. "I'll be a somebody. Just think what we can do with this place when I get the pay rise." He leaps out of bed, flinging back the blankets. I let out a cry as the cold air swirls around my torso. He slaps the on button for the single lamp we own. The bulb flickers before sending its weak glow throughout our tiny shelter. "I will make us a home."

I sit up, blinking, pulling the blankets up around me. "Dimi, what are you—?"

"A *proper* fireplace." He runs over to the crumbling, decrepit fireplace that is never lit, the chimney stuffed full of newspaper to battle against the cold seeping in. "I'll build you a huge fireplace, one that works, with a thick mantle and a stack of firewood taller than you, so you'll never be cold."

I giggle as he jumps across the room.

"And here! Here I'll put your new desk so you can do your schoolwork."

"And write," I add.

Dimi nods, the impossible realities of my dream forgotten as he loses himself in his own. "A proper wooden desk. And stacks of paper with lines. And pens. Lots of pens. I'll buy you a large, comfortable chair so you don't hurt your back sitting cramped over your homework in your lap." His eyes dart across to another wall. "And bookcases!"

I laugh and clap my hands as he dances around with all the enthusiasm of a child, painting our dreams over this dirty hovel with his hands. His voice gets louder and louder, so I'm sure our neighbours have woken up too. He is unrestrained and wild. He is fire and passion. And I love him for it.

He runs to our old vinyl record player, the one we scavenged from a dump site. We couldn't believe anyone would throw away something so precious. We only have one record, "Stormy Weather" by Billie Holiday. The slow jazz music blares out at full volume, Billie's voice crooning through the air.

"Dimi! Our neighbours!"

"Let them dance too." He grabs my hand, pulling me up to my feet. "Dance with me."

"You lunatic," I cry with a laugh, "it's almost midnight."

"An even better reason to dance, then. For if you dance well enough at midnight," he says, repeating the beginning of an old folk tale for the hundredth time.

"…the fairies will grant you a wish," I finish for him.

I wish…

For good food—enough food—and warm furs. For a desk and a working fireplace.

I squeeze my eyes shut and I wish with every cell of my being as the music turns us round and round.

After the song dies and there's just a crackle, we're still swaying in each other's arms.

He lowers his forehead to mine. "I love you, Alena. I want to give you everything. Everything your heart desires. Everything you deserve."

My heart clenches. He calls me the dreamer, but I think, between the two of us, he is more of that than me. "I know," I say quietly.

He crushes his lips to mine, kissing me long and deep, with the fire of a new-born sun, his tongue fighting with mine. My head keeps spinning even as we stop twirling. And I forget everything.

We are no longer two poor, pathetic wretches on the edge of starvation, uncared for and forgotten. We are stars and light tumbling between the moon and sun. We are wild and free.

Chapter Three

Dimitri

Alena and I tumble onto the bed, my body filling to bursting as I kiss her. I'm swollen and desperate with love and fire and the overwhelming need to protect her. If only I could wrap her up in cotton and keep her safe. If only I could hide her from the bitter unfairness of the world. If only I could give her everything her generous heart desires.

I want to see her radiating with happiness, to see her thin girlish figure fill out with healthy soft curves because she has enough to eat. She is skinny now. Too skinny. Every time my hands brush over her protruding hip bones, I feel the stab of failure. Despite that, she is still the most stunning creature in the world. I want her. I *need* her.

I stiffen as her soft tongue dances with mine, lust burning a trail through me. My hand slips under her shirt and I find her warm belly. She lets out a gasp but she doesn't pull away. She presses closer to me, her kisses growing wilder, her fingers tugging at my hair. My hand trails up, up to brush the underside of her budding breasts.

Stop it, Dimi. She's only fifteen.

I snatch my hand off her and tear my lips off hers. She groans, a mirror of my body crying out to touch her again.

"Why did you stop?" Alena pouts, and it takes every fibre of my willpower not to take her bottom lip into my mouth and suck.

"You know why," I say, my breathing heavy. I struggle to control myself—my breath, my hands, my need.

She sighs. "Because I'm not even sixteen yet."

"And I'm nineteen."

"But I turn sixteen in seven days. Is seven days really going to make a difference?"

"Yes."

"No one's going to turn you in for taking a minor's virginity." Her face screws up. "My parents certainly don't give a shit. They don't care if I'm alive or dead."

I let out a low curse. "It's not about the law."

She rolls her eyes. "I know. I know. It's about your damn morals." Despite being annoyed at me, she honours me with one of her half-smiles. "It's one of the reasons I love you, you know? You'd never take advantage of me." She stares at me through her long lashes and chews on her full bottom lip. She looks almost shy when she does it. The shyness is a ruse.

I let out a groan as she presses her soft body against me, slipping one leg in between mine so her core presses right up against me. Fuck. I can feel her soft heat through our clothes. I grit my teeth. "You make it so hard for me to stick to my damn morals."

She giggles. "I know." She grinds herself against my thigh and my dick throbs.

I curse. My fingers grip onto her hips, unsure whether to stop her or urge her on. "You enjoy torturing me."

"You torture me too," she says in a breathless whisper, her breathing growing heavy as she continues to rock her core against me. "I'm so...wet. I want you so fucking bad."

Jesus Christ. Those dirty words coming off her tongue, out of her innocent plump mouth, sends another aching pulse through me.

"Alena, stop," I beg. She has to stop. I can't stop her.

She's too far gone.

I can do nothing but watch as the thunder shudders through her, the lightning snapping her fingers into fists in my shirt. Her lashes flutter closed, shutting off those hypnotic green eyes. I can smell her desire, thick in the air like summer rain. God, how I want to taste it. I want to lick every last drop. Her pink mouth drops open and a siren's cry releases from inside her. She is the most stunning creature I have ever seen.

I'm a mass of coiled, painful tension as I watch her come down from the pleasure I am not allowing myself to enjoy with her yet. I'm shaking, my fingers gripping her like claws.

Seven more days.

I've waited so long for her. Seven days shouldn't be so hard. But for some reason these seven days feel painfully swollen out towards eternity.

Stay strong, Dimi.

Her eyes flutter open. Once again I am trapped in her stare. I can see by the way she chews her bottom lip she expects me to be angry with her.

"That was so fucking beautiful," I whisper.

She smiles and reaches down between us for my aching dick. For a second I almost let her. If I do, I can kiss good-fucking-bye to my morals. I grab her wrist and hold her hand away, attempting a stern look.

She pouts. "I just want to make it good for you, too."

"You do."

Her frown deepens. "But you won't even let me make you come."

That's because I know if she touches me, I'll give in and take everything. I'll let myself sink into her precious untouched folds. "You will. Sixteen is only seven days away."

She sighs. "I guess."

I smile at her and rub my nose along hers. "Besides, the first time I come with you, it'll be inside you. You'll be able to *feel* me, to watch me fall apart."

She shudders and her tiny pink tongue slides out to wet her bottom lip. That little move has my dick screaming.

Mother Russia, give me strength.

I shuffle her to face the other way before I lose all control, and tuck her against me with a delicate touch as if she is made of porcelain. When she shivers again my lungs squeeze so hard that it hurts. She is my everything. My heart. My breath. My sun and spring.

I think of the box I have hidden away for her birthday and the demure white lace inside it. She said once that she'd love to know what having pretty, matching underwear felt like. I splurged and bought them on sale from one of those specialty shops. It wasn't every day that a girl became a woman. I want to make it perfect for her. So fucking perfect.

Shit, I have to stop thinking of my lamb in white lace panties or else I'll lose my mind.

She coughs, the sound sharp and dry. My fingers dig into her side.

"Alena?" I say, worry clear in my voice.

"I'm fine. Just...something in my throat."

She's lying. She's getting sick. She's getting sick and I need to keep her warm. But our tiny studio apartment, no insulation, single-paned windows, in a near-derelict building is so expensive to heat. We need to get out of Russia. Somewhere warmer. Anywhere warmer. Somewhere where two unskilled teens can find work. I squeeze my eyes shut and imagine a large stone woman in robes holding a torch in her hand. America. The land of opportunity. The land of the free. One day we'll get to see the great lady statue greeting us on our arrival.

I think back to the pathetic slip of rubles I have hidden behind a vent. That's my get-the-fuck-out-of-here fund. At the moment, there is only enough for one plane ticket to America plus change. For the last few months I've barely added to it. I'm doing my best. But my best is never good enough.

Anger curls in my gut. *Hello, my old friend.* Sometimes I'm not even sure why I'm angry, I just know that I am. I'm angry at God for bestowing such shitty lives to Alena and me. I'm angry because it seems that no matter how hard I work at the factory, I can't seem to get ahead. I'm angry that this piece of shit government doesn't care about us. I hate that there are always more bills to pay. Rent. Food. Heating. Electricity. School books. Clothes. On and fucking on.

We still need more money. I can't use the money I have saved to pay for heating this coming winter. We need it to leave, to make a better life for us both.

If Alena freezes to death there won't be any life for either of you, you stupid boy, the sharp voice of my dead mother says in my head.

My heart cracks at the thought of losing Alena. I can't. I would die. I grip her tighter to me, clinging to her as if it could stop her from ever leaving.

We're going to have to take another risk. One more risk. One more score. One that is big enough to get us both out of here and to a better life.

Chapter Four

Alena

St Petersburg is a city of extremes. Grey blocks of communist apartments like prisons right next to cathedrals with soaring domes like fat rings on the end of fingers and palaces built of solid marble peopled with kneeling virgins and weeping angels.

I wandered through the Peterhof Palace once on a school trip. The floors were inlaid with precious and exotic woods, the soaring hand-painted ceiling cast with enough gold leaf that gold dust shone in the air, making the streaks of light that came through the tall windows gleam. There is so much opulence in a city of the desperate that it makes me sick.

In summer, walking along the Griboedov Canal at night when the sun barely dips under the horizon's surface like a seagull snatching up fish, the air takes on a magical light. It glistens off the jewelled domes of the Church of Our Savior on the Spilled Blood and dances over the golden dragons that line the Bank Bridge. It's on one of these white nights that I believe the world is full of magic. That wishes can be bought with the light of the stars. That dreams are more than mist and smoke.

Dimitri says I'm a romantic. He warns me, half-jokingly, that I live in the clouds, that my dreams are held together with wax. It will melt one day and I'll come crashing down to the earth like Icarus.

In winter, the city is suffocated by the low-hanging grey woollen sky. The air is as sharp as daggers and the thick layer of snow covers the patches of ice underneath lying in wait to send you to your knees. I envy the couples walking hand in hand, wrapped tight in their real mink, sable or polar furs and valenki felt boots. My clothes are all second-hand and ill-fitting. I want to sit in one of those plush chairs in a warm, glowing penthouse and lift a glass of sparkling wine and toast to my charmed life.

As I walk into the bar of the Kempinski Hotel, a luxury riverside hotel set in a nineteenth century mansion, my stomach tumbles with nerves and bitterness. The smell of spiced wine and money doesn't help. Nor does the sombre Russian rock ballad humming from the speakers in the ceiling, "My Heart" by *KIT-I*.

Part of me doesn't want to take this risk again. The other part thinks that it's one little way that Dimitri and I can tip the unfair balance a little towards us. Our desperate lives have been so unfairly dealt to us.

I'm wearing a simple black knee-length dress and black stockings under an overly large fur coat, both stolen. As are my black boots, two sizes too large for me so that I have to wear three pairs of thick socks just so they don't clomp when I walk. I'd never get into a place as fancy as this if I wore my own clothes, another bitter thought. I don't own any makeup. I've smudged ash around my eyes to make them pop and pinched my cheeks to make them rosy. It's the best I can do.

I shrug my coat off my shoulders and drape it over one arm. They're so generous with the heating in here that I have a small bead of sweat on my upper lip.

I spot Dimitri, making my breath catch in my throat. He is stunning in a dark grey suit, also stolen. Luckily for him, the suit is his size, showing off his broad shoulders and slim waist. His dark hair is pushed back off his strong forehead, his blue eyes like chips of ice against the dark frame of thick lashes.

He's leaning against the bar, chatting to a woman clothed in a white tailored pantsuit, a daring choice of attire here in traditionalist Russia. She must be foreign. She has dark hair coiffed into a stylish twist, so complex and perfect that she couldn't have possibly done it herself. Foreign, and too pompous to do her own damn hair.

My steps are surer as I wind my way towards them, taking a languid route through the glossy tables and chairs so as not to appear to be aiming for them. As I near, I catch her voice and a lilt of an accent. She's speaking Russian with what sounds like an American accent.

Dimitri catches my eye over her shoulder. He pulls the woman closer to him and lowers his mouth to her ear as if to whisper something. A stab of jealousy goes through me. I shove it down. Dimitri is just acting. He's pretending to want her. He's not drawing her closer, he's drawing her farther away from her purse, a fat white leather clutch, sitting forgotten on the bar stool behind her.

The bar stool I am almost upon.

My steps are light and quick. Dimitri says something to her and she laughs loudly, her hands all over his chest, forcing me to fight another stab of pain. This was *my* plan, after all. Dimitri was always better at being charming and distracting. And she's totally distracted. I am barely breathing as I hold my coat beside me to hide my actions. I reach for her purse and—

A large, firm hand grips my upper arm, sending a jolt through me. I let go of the clutch and it falls to the floor with a clatter.

Everything seems to stop. Even the music. I look up and a huge man in a suit with hair cut close to his skull is gripping me, glaring at me.

Oh my God. I've been busted.

"What's going on?" the woman says in her accented Russian as she turns her back on Dimitri.

I suck in a breath as her eyes lock onto mine, her irises as dark as crows' feathers. Her skin glows with the perfect amount of blush, her lashes thick and lush. Her deep red lipstick matches her perfectly manicured nails. I can smell her expensive woodsy perfume wafting seductively in the air, not too light, not too heavy. Her ears drip with diamond chandelier earrings that brush against her collarbones. Her fingers glint with more jewels, all costing more money than I'll ever know in my entire life. I'm filled with a sudden hateful rage, my fingers digging into my palms. She's everything that I want to be but am not. Why does she deserve to have everything while I have nothing?

Behind her, another large man in a suit grabs Dimitri by the elbows, locking them behind his back. Dimitri is strong, but he's no match for the overfed bulldog holding him.

She has bodyguards? Who the hell did Dimitri pick as a mark?

The woman says something in English to the man holding me hostage. From what little I've learned in school, I pick up the words "purse" and "thief".

Shit. We're so screwed.

I attempt to appear indignant, like I'm just another rich, entitled princess, as I demand to be let go. I claim it was just an accident that my coat caught the edge of her purse and knocked it over.

The woman doesn't buy it. I can see it in the way she narrows her eyes at me. Dimitri demands to be let go as well, but it's not helping.

"Both of you shut up or I'll call the authorities," she commands in Russian.

Dimitri and I fall silent at the word *authorities*. We catch each other's gaze and when I look back, the woman is looking at me, nodding slightly. She knows Dimitri and I have been working together. She waves off the hotel manager, who has rushed over to see what the problem is.

"I have this under control," she says, and refocuses her eyes on me.

Her look suddenly changes. She studies me, eyeing me up and down my entire body. I feel stripped. I've never felt so scrutinized. She hums under her breath. "You have real potential. Even in stolen rags you are..." she lifts her onyx eyes up to drill into mine, "stunning."

I feel a chill settle down my spine. A series of thoughts runs through my head.

How the hell could she tell that my dress and coat were stolen?

Potential? For what?

She flicks her hand towards the bodyguard holding Dimitri. "Take him outside," she says. "I want to have a word with her. Alone." Her eyes remain steadily on me.

"No," Dimitri cries out, ripping my attention to him as the bulldog drags him away. "Let her go."

"Dimitri!" I struggle to free myself of my captor, but he's too strong, gripping my arm tighter until I wince. The woman's hand comes down on mine, startling me. It is soft and supple. She has never done an hour of real work in her life.

"I promise he won't be harmed," she says, her voice like honeyed poison. "If you don't want me to go to the police and tell them of your little scam, then you'll give me two minutes of your time."

Two minutes.

I feel the gravity in her request, the unseen weight. I sense these two minutes have the potential to affect everything.

"I won't leave her alone with you." Dimitri elbows the man holding him, causing a grunt to burst from him. He's almost free.

"Stop!" I cry. "Let me hear what she has to say."

A flash of betrayal thunders across his face. He doesn't try to hide it. He's never been good at hiding how he feels. "Alena—"

"Just two minutes, Dimi," I say in that soft voice I know brings him to his knees. "Please."

Dimitri's eyes are fixed on me, his dark brows furrowed in disapproval. "I don't trust her."

"I don't either. But I don't want us to end up in jail." I'm not entirely truthful. I am desperate to know what the woman has to say. The way she said that I had *potential* makes me...hopeful. She's the only one who's ever seen *anything* more in me except for Dimitri. I can feel her gaze on me. It might be my imagination, but she seems pleased.

I know I've won when Dimitri's shoulders fall. "Two minutes." He glares at the woman and repeats himself. "Two minutes, or else I'm coming back in here for her."

Dimitri shrugs out of the bulldog's grasp and storms out of the hotel bar. The hair on my neck stands on end the way it does when I know he's looking at me. When I look over my shoulder, he's glaring at us through the front windows as he paces back and forth, the night wind whipping his hair around.

The bodyguard releases his grip on my arm and moves to stand at a respectable distance away at the end of the bar. So does the other bulldog. I am left with *her*.

Her eyes have not left my face, a smile toying at the corner of her lush, painted lips. "Alena, is it? You look young. Eighteen? Nineteen?"

"Eighteen," I lie. I don't want to get into any more trouble for being underage. "You said I had potential. Potential for what?"

"My name is Isabelle. I manage an agency. An international agency with offices worldwide."

I straighten. "A modelling agency?" Models make money. Real money. They're clothed and adored and everybody loves them. Could I be a model? I always thought I was just an inch too short.

"Something more…exclusive than modelling. Tell me, Alena, are you a virgin?"

"Y-you can't ask me that," I stutter, my cheeks growing hot.

Her smile widens even further. "I thought so. How sweet."

Sweet? She's mocking me. I'm so flustered that I can't speak.

Isabelle looks over my shoulder, where I know Dimitri is still watching us. "Then I take it he's *not* your boyfriend? Despite how much he wants to be."

Boyfriend? Boyfriend feels like such a juvenile word to describe what Dimitri and I are to each other. I don't answer her question. "What do you want?"

She smiles, her perfect red lips parting to reveal a set of

straight white teeth. For some reason, they look wolfish. "I have an offer for you that will change your life."

Chapter Five

The present…

I close the box, my breath shuddering through my teeth, my lungs feeling shredded.

Enough.

That's enough of these sharp memories right now.

I fold each thing back into the cavity and lock the box, before slipping the key back into my locket and hiding the locket back under my clothing. I stand at the side of my bed, about to bend down to slip it back out of sight, when my door bursts open with a bang against the wall.

"Alena," Emily's high-pitched voice calls as she bounds into my room.

I quickly slip the box onto my side table and hope it is camouflaged among the elaborate vintage lamp and small pile of books I've borrowed from the manor library. I'll have to tuck it away later.

I turn towards Emily. She looks like her father, the same straight chestnut hair, milk-and-cream skin, same deep-set grey eyes. Except her face is sweet and round, and her father's is all shrunken cheeks and pointed chin. She's only three years younger than me at eighteen, my husband's daughter from his previous wife, now dead.

"Emily, you're up." She's already dressed for the day in a long grey knit dress and semi-opaque stockings, a pair of ballet flats on her feet. I'm still in my silk dressing gown, my nightgown underneath.

"What shall we do today?" she asks.

Her smile is infectious. I feel myself dusting off all these old cobwebs. Emily is the one good thing in my life. The one joy. "Don't you have a music lesson today? With Mrs Prim?"

She gives me a guilty look. "Um, she might have yelled at me last time, telling me that I was an untalented brat and that she was never coming back."

"And what did you do to make her lash out like that?"

"Nothing." The innocence in her face cracks. "Okay, so I may have told her that I didn't want to do her boring old scales."

I snort. "That should do it."

"Besides, I will never be able to play the piano the way Father wants me to."

"Because you won't practice your scales."

She screws up her face. "I swear she had a flute stuck up her ass."

"Surely having something up your bum would make you a more pleasant person."

"Alena!" Emily admonishes me, her cheeks blushing furiously.

Despite myself, I laugh. "Let's go steal Mrs Bates' work gloves and throw them up a tree." Mrs Bates is the crotchety old housekeeper. She can't stand Emily and me, and we return the favour. It probably doesn't help matters that we play tricks on her when we're bored.

"Oooh, no, let's act out one of your stories! Have you written any new ones?"

"Um, not recently." I'm lying. I have been working on a story, a new story, but I don't want to share it. It's too personal. Too raw. It's taken me five years just to be able to start writing it down.

I do have lots of things to be grateful for. I never go hungry. We have a cook who lives with us on-site. I am never cold. I have real fur cloaks and this place is well heated. We even have real fireplaces; some rooms have two. I have a small study down the hall, just for me, with my own desk that I always wanted, with lots of pens and paper and…

There's just something missing. Some*one* missing.

Emily frowns at me, her eyes sliding past me towards my bedside table. "What's that? I've never seen that before."

My jaw tightens. I know exactly what's she's looking at. "Seen what?"

"That box." Emily strides past me before I can stop her. "It doesn't look like it belongs here." She's right. The simple box sticks out among all this elaborate, fussy luxury. She walks right to it and grabs it. The sight of my box in someone else's hand makes my chest seize. I stop breathing for a second. It takes all of my willpower not to snatch the box from her grubby little hands. I almost cry when she shakes it, the contents rattling like dice in a cup. "What's inside?"

My fingers flinch as I restrain myself from snatching it from her. The bigger deal I make out of it, the more Emily won't leave it alone. "It's nothing," I say, trying to keep my voice steady and casual. I fail.

"There's something in there. I can hear it."

I let out a curt, humourless laugh as I wave it off. "It's been so long, I've forgotten what's inside."

"Let's open it."

"You can't!"

"Why not?"

"I've...lost the key."

Emily looks at me, a tiny crease between her brows. "Then why do you keep it?"

I shrug even as the pain lances me like someone has fisted the broken edges of the contents of the box into my chest. "It's the only thing I have left from my life before here." These are true words. And they are swollen with pain.

Emily's frown deepens, sadness pulling down the corners of her mouth, adding to my guilt. "I thought we were friends, best friends."

"We are." She's my only friend. She has been for five years.

"Then why won't you tell me what's inside?"

"There's nothing to tell," I snap. *Leave it alone, you selfish girl. This is mine. Only mine.*

Her face darkens. She knows I'm lying. "Best friends tell each other everything."

Now I feel terrible. Terrible for lying. Terrible for my hateful thoughts towards her.

And yet, a part of me is dying to tell. Dying to unwrap this throbbing wound that has never closed. Perhaps it's time to share my secret shame, my hidden grief. Perhaps it's time to unburden myself to someone.

Perhaps I can trust Emily with my greatest mistake.

I take a step towards her. My footing goes as something sharp lances through my lower belly. I gasp and press at my stomach.

Oh God. Please, no.

"Leni?" she says, leaving the box now forgotten on the table and stretches her hands out towards me. "Are you okay?"

The ache throbs again, this time sharper. I let out a cry and double over, clutching at my stomach. This feels just like the last time. "No," I gasp, my lungs seizing as panic grips me.

"Leni!"

Pain lashes through me in waves. My vision blurs behind tears. Breathe. Can't breathe. I feel myself falling into a well of pain.

Everything goes black.

Chapter Six

Alena

Five years ago…

"Abso-fucking-lutly not." Dimitri's voice grinds out between his clenched teeth.

After we leave the Kempinski Hotel bar, I wait until we get back to our apartment to tell him about Isabelle's offer. I know this is not a conversation we should have in public.

"I know it's unorthodox," I say softly. "But just think about it."

Dimitri begins to pace across our threadbare carpet, his hands yanking through his hair. "I can't believe you're even entertaining the thought of marrying some stranger for money."

"It is not for money, it is for *us*." I grab his shoulders, causing him to stop pacing and forcing him to look at me. "For *us*, Dimi."

He pushes my hands off me, as if my touch burns him. "Don't you *dare* say this is for us. I don't want this."

"You don't want this?" I yell back, frustration turning in my gut. Here is a once-in-a-lifetime opportunity, handed to us on a platter, and he isn't even considering it. "You don't want a better life? You want to starve? To freeze to death?"

"Of course I want a better life. But not like this."

"Then how—?"

"You are not a fucking whore!" he screams, making the window panes shudder.

His words slap me in my face. That was one aspect I hadn't really thought through. If I married a stranger, I'd have to…

I shove that thought down into the dark pit of my mind. That is something I can deal with later. I hadn't even been made an offer from any potential wealthy husbands yet. I have just been given the offer to sign up with Isabelle's agency. Even if I sign up, I may not get chosen by anyone.

I only realise I'm shaking when Dimitri wraps his strong arms around me. "Oh, Alena," he whispers in my hair, "I'm sorry for yelling. Just the thought of you with another man…it *kills* me." He presses a kiss to my forehead and sighs.

I melt into his arms, letting his warmth wrap around me until it's just him and me. We are stronger than anything.

"It's just an offer, Dimi," I say. "Just something for us to consider."

"The answer's no."

Resentment swirls around in my gut. He hasn't even considered it properly.

"Promise me you won't go back to Isabelle," he says.

I squeeze my eyes shut as the backs of them sting. Visions of a better life that Isabelle had built up earlier crumble before me—of a life of never being cold, of never feeling the angry gnaw of hunger in my belly, of never having to beg or steal for what I want. I want a better life so badly. So, so badly. Desperation tears me up inside.

"Alena?"

What's the harm in just seeing what could come of this? It's not like I have to say "yes"…

Dimitri pulls back to look at me. I don't want to fight with him right now. I can't tell him I'm going to sign up. Not yet. *I'm doing this for us*, I tell myself. He'll come around once he sees the real opportunity on offer. If there even is an offer…

"I promise," I lie, fingers crossed behind my back.

Chapter Seven

Dimitri

Alena is lying to me.

I know because her school called me at the factory yesterday to tell me that she has missed school for the third day in a row. They think I'm her guardian because we forged the papers.

I should have known something was up. She's been distant these last few days, her eyes skipping past me to stare into nothing but blank space more often than not, her lips moving as I kiss her but the fire behind it as low as coals. I've just been so busy...

She's been distant...since the run-in with Isabelle. There's a hollowness digging a pit in my stomach. She's never lied to me before.

I don't confront her. Instead I pretend to go to work as usual even though it's my rostered day off. I wait around the corner from our crumbling brick apartment building.

Finally, she appears at the front door of our building. Her hair looks thick and styled as it tumbles over her fur coat, the same fur coat she wore when we met Isabelle. I squint as she steps out into the grey morning. Is that…? Her eyes are done up and she has red lipstick on her mouth. She has makeup on, *real* makeup. Where did she get makeup from?

My stomach drops. I think I know where she's going.

I hang back, watching her stride down the street a decent distance before I follow her, my collar pulled up around my jaw. Her walk is different. Her hips sway like she's suddenly become aware of them and the power they hold. The way she's holding her shoulders is different, thrown back to showcase her blooming chest. Men blatantly check her out, heads turning as she walks past them, weaving her way through St Petersburg. A group of men call out obscenities to her from across the street, grabbing their dicks and thrusting. My vision bleeds. *She's just a child*, I want to scream. It takes every inch of my willpower not to run over there and beat the living shit out of every single one of them.

The Alena-who-doesn't-look-like-my-Alena continues on. And on. Until she stops at the black painted door of a six-storey grey Gothic building trimmed with stonework arches, all the windows at the front looking out like dead black eyes.

On the doorstep, Alena presses the buzzer and fluffs her hair as she waits. The door opens. My gut twists as I watch her disappear inside.

I wait a few excruciating seconds before I sneak up to the door. There's a single buzzer with just two taunting letters against it:

GW

Isabelle's agency. My worst fucking nightmare. Dear God. What are they doing to her in there?

I get a flash in my mind of Alena inside, stripped to her underwear, a collar around her neck, being paraded up and down a row of old seedy, grabby men like some kind of sick dog show. Sit. Stay. Roll over...

Something snaps inside me. My vision bleeds red. I'm slamming my fist against the door before I know what I'm doing. "Alena," I scream. I keep banging, the door reverberating in its frame, my voice going hoarse from calling her name. I'm going to beat this fucking door down if someone doesn't open it soon.

The door swings open. I barely notice the wide-eyed woman standing in the doorway. "Can I help—?"

She jumps out of my way as I barge past her, stepping into a stylish lobby area of white and cream. There is a cluster of girls, all young, all pretty, crowding around the top of a set of stairs, whispering to each other and watching me with startled doe eyes.

"Where's Alena?" I demand.

The whispers heighten and they glance around at each other.

I grind my teeth. "Where is she? I know she's in here."

"Dimitri?" Alena's voice calls over the murmuring. Her voice sends another wave of fury through me. The crowd parts and she appears on the top step, her features morphing somewhere between mortified and furious.

Frankly, I don't give a shit that she's embarrassed.

"It's okay," she says to the bleating ninnies around her. "He's my brother."

Her brother?

I stomp up the stairs, sending some of the girls scattering. Alena races down to meet me halfway. "What the hell are you doing here?" she hisses.

"I should ask *you* the same fucking question."

"Let's talk somewhere else, Dimi. Please." Alena glances over her shoulder. She's nervous. She's afraid that we're making a scene.

The scene hasn't fucking started yet.

A wave of madness comes over me. I tackle her around the waist and hoist her over my shoulder, setting off a round of gasps. I spin, careful not to bang her against the wall, and carry her down the stairs.

"What the fuck are you doing?" She beats at my back and kicks at the air but I am too damn furious to feel anything. I am numb with fury. I'm practically vibrating with rage. "Put me down."

I storm out the door, no one daring to stop me. "No fucking chance, sweetheart."

Chapter Eight

Alena

The present…

I wake reluctantly, because in my dreams is where Dimitri lives. I'm a fish on a hook being dragged ever closer to the surface, while I struggle to remain in the murky depths where my heart and my secrets lie like sunken treasures.

The surface breaks over me in a wash of light behind my closed lids. I open them and blink at the figure sitting at my side. Emily's worried face comes into focus. She lets out a sigh of relief. "Thank goodness. I was so worried."

I'm in my bed, in my room. It's dim. My curtains are closed but the bedside lamp is on. The air smells stale and there's a sharp scent of disinfectant and something coppery underneath.

A shadow moves behind Emily and I realise we're not alone. Standing behind her is Mrs Bates, the head housekeeper, a woman with a face like she's permanently sucking on a lemon. She must be at least fifty, given the amount of crow's feet around her tiny black eyes that I always seem to catch glaring at me, her hair pulled back into a severe bun at the nape of her stringy neck. She wears her usual uniform of solemn dark colours, her skirt skimming the floor.

"What happened?" I ask automatically. My throat is dry as sandpaper. I wince as the rest of my body cries out. There's a dull ache in my lower belly. My hand flies to the surface where the pain is radiating from. I feel wet between my legs. Soaking.

I don't need to hear what happened. I know.

I know.

Emily doesn't answer right away. She helps me sit up, rearranging my pillows behind me, then hands me a glass of water. When I'm finished, she places the empty glass well away from me, as if she knows to keep anything breakable out of my reach. "The doctor's been here."

I look down. They laid towels underneath me. Towels.

"I'm so sorry, Leni," she says, her voice taking on a soft, hesitant tone. "The doctor said that these things happen, sometimes for no reason. There was nothing he could—"

"You lost the baby," Mrs Bates blurts out. Her words hang disjointed and sharp in the air. I try not to breathe them in, but there's no denying reality when it's a fog around you.

"Mrs Bates," admonishes Emily.

"What?" There is no apology in Mrs Bates' look. "Better she hears it straight. Not the way you were faffing about."

Emily turns her back on Mrs Bates with an exasperated sigh. The instant her gaze falls on me, her features soften into a look of pity. "I'm so sorry," she says, her voice warbling. Her eyes fill with tears as she grips my limp hand.

"No use in dwelling on these things," Mrs Bates says.

Emily stiffens. She hates Mrs Bates as much as I do. But it doesn't matter what we think. She's been working for my husband longer than Emily has been alive. He'll never fire her. "Leave us, please."

"I've got to—"

"That's an order, Mrs Bates." Emily's voice is as firm as I've ever heard it, causing a small thread of pride to go through me. Usually she's too passive and obliging.

Mrs Bates opens her mouth, probably to argue again. Thankfully she chooses not to and snaps it shut, grunting as she turns away. "I'll be back to change the sheets." The door clicks shut behind her.

"Leni?" Emily's soft voice breaks through my haze. "Are you okay?"

Am I okay?

No.

I force a smile and try for a nod. I can't let her see how broken I am.

"Did…did you know you were pregnant?" I can hear the real question underneath her words. Did I keep this a secret from her?

There are so many things she doesn't have the strength to know. "I didn't want to jinx it, you know?" I say, my voice scraping against the back of my throat. "The last time…" I trail off. The first two times I fell pregnant, I was so happy I couldn't help but share the news. "Turns out I jinxed it anyway."

The corners of Emily's lips pull down. "Leni, you know that's not true." Her platitude sounds hollow and fake. The truth is, I am jinxed.

My prison bars thicken around me as the true weight of what has happened hits me like a fist to the stomach. I fall back onto my pillow, covering my aching eyes with my arm. My jaw stings but I refuse to cry.

I refuse.

"Leni—?"

"I just want to be alone. Please."

There's a small pause. "I'm sorry. So sorry." The edge of the mattress shifts as she stands. Her soft footfalls sound across my room. My door is opened, then shut. Then deafening silence.

I can't help but think as I lie here in the dim, that I deserved this. The third miscarriage in five years. I thought three was a lucky number. Third time's the charm, isn't that what they say in English?

Perhaps this is God's way of punishing me. Perhaps this is my body's way of punishing me.

So be it. I deserve it.

A broken heart in exchange for the heart I broke…

Chapter Nine

Alena

Five years ago...

Dimitri kicks open the door to our apartment, me still over his shoulder. He dumps me on the carpet where I immediately retreat a few steps, just to get some space from him. I am breathless, my throat raw from screaming at him, my hands bruised from beating at his back. He kicks the door shut behind him with a bang.

He stands there, glaring at me, a vein in his temple throbbing. His hands are tight fists at his side. He's more furious than I've ever seen him. His eyes have become two whirlpools, anger and disbelief frothing in those dark blue depths. I suck in a breath, preparing myself to yell at him for the way he just manhandled me.

"You lied to me." The pain in his voice slides under my skin like a splinter.

Guilt cuts a hole in the bottom of me and the fight drains out of me. It's the first time I've ever lied to him.

I should have told him I had signed up with Isabelle's agency. I should have told him I was going to their grooming and deportment classes. But I knew he wouldn't have let me go. I just wanted to see what would happen. I just wanted to know what the possibilities were. I shift, uneasy on my feet. "I was going to tell you."

"When?" he barks out, making me wince.

My stomach churns as a seed of doubt weaves through my mind. Am I doing the right thing?

Be brave, Alena, I tell myself. I did this because I want a better life for *us*. He's angry because he doesn't know how good this opportunity is. I just have to make him see. "I was going to tell you tonight. Isabelle made me an offer…"

Dimitri's nostrils flare.

I barrel on before he can speak. "There's a wealthy gentleman. He's English. He picked me out. Me, specifically."

His lip curls up. "Let me get this straight." His voice is low and deadly. "You want to marry a man who picked you out of a fucking line-up?"

I wince at his curses. He hardly ever curses in front of me. He thinks it's rude and disrespectful.

Do I want to marry this stranger? Of course not. I love Dimitri. I've loved Dimitri from the moment I set eyes on him two years ago. I don't want to marry a stranger. But I want what this marriage provides *us*.

I don't want to starve anymore. I don't want to freeze. I want a better life. More than anything. I want it so badly it hurts. I want it so badly I can taste it.

"We get five million pounds. Five million, Dimi, can you even imagine that?" Five million pounds. My head still spins with this number. It means good food. A proper place to live. A ticket out of Russia. We need this. We have a chance at a better life and I will take it for us even if he is not brave enough. I will hate myself forever if I give up this opportunity.

Dimitri's face has turned to stone. He says nothing so I keep going. "I've had you written into the contract. You'll come with us to England, live with us. You see, I told them you're my brother."

He doesn't react. I think it's sinking in. I think he's coming around. There's just one tiny bit that might be hard for him to swallow.

"All I have to do is…give birth to a son." Dimitri's eyes flare, his breath coming in short, hard bursts. He's like a pot about to overboil. He's trying not to explode. I move towards him, palms out, speaking fast. "I'll make sure that he gets wild cotton in his food so his sperm count will drop. Don't worry, the baby will be *ours*. Once we have the five million, we can disappear, you and me and our baby, to America like we always dreamed." I slide my hands onto his arms, begging him with my eyes to see the vision dancing before us. A wonderful life. No more worries. No more suffering. He can start his own company. I can write. "We'll be rich. We'll never have to worry about anything again." No more stealing. No more scams. No more desperation.

His jaw twitches. "And if you break the contract? If he finds out you're *fucking* your 'brother' before you deliver him a boy?"

My hands drop from his arms. The one tiny snag, the tiny thing that makes me nervous, and he's found it. The "conduct unbecoming of a good wife" clause, triggered if

I leave him or if I'm unfaithful. "I'll owe him the cost of what he paid for me," I say in a whisper. "And forfeit the five million."

Disbelief cracks through his mask. A deep sadness oozes out. The way he stares at me feels like acid under my skin. It burns and scars. "Do you love me, Alena?"

I gasp. "Of course I love you."

"You know I love you."

"Of course, I—"

"Then tell me, *my love*," his voice begins to rise, "how can I be okay with you *marrying* a total stranger? How can you expect me to stand idly by while your new husband *fucks* you?"

I wince. It's just my body. Dimitri will always have my heart and my soul. Doesn't he know that? "How is it any different from when we run our scams? You're the one who pretends to be interested in those stupid women so we can steal from them. How is this any different?"

"I'm not marrying them," Dimitri explodes. "I'm not fucking them and I'm not getting them pregnant."

My heart cracks as my future cracks apart. My charmed life blurs before my eyes. Why is he trying to take this away from me? From us?

Dimitri drops to his knees in front of me. His face cracks wide open, but it's not anger showing through, raw and naked.

It's desperation.

"Alena," he grabs my hand, "I beg of you, don't do this."

"Dimi, I—"

"Don't marry him, marry me." His eyes glisten with tears. "I don't have a ring now but I will get one. I will. I can give you everything you've ever wanted. I promise, just…"

I squeeze my eyes shut, tears spilling out. I have imagined this moment for so long, Dimi on his knees asking me to be his wife. But not like this. Not like this. He's only asking me to try to blackmail me into giving up my dream. Screw him, he's spitting on our love by doing this.

I open my eyes, my heart turning to ice, and tug my hand from his. "Get up. You look ridiculous on the floor."

He leaps to his feet, his eyes going wild and terrible. His finger shakes as he stabs it in my chest. "I took you in." Stab. "I cared for you after you were abandoned by your mother." Stab. "And this is how you repay me?"

"Repay you?" I slap his hand away from me. "I'm trying to make a life for us."

"That is what *I'm* doing!"

"No, Dimitri, this isn't a fucking life. This is death. We are dying, slowly. *I* am dying. And you. Are. Killing me."

I see the moment when his heart breaks. I can almost hear when his pride snaps in two. Shit. I've gone too far. I regret everything I said. Everything. I take it back.

But I can't. My words have done their damage. Like lightning cleaving a tree in half.

"Get out," he spits out between his teeth.

I reach out for him. "Dimi—"

"Don't fucking touch me, you whore."

His words slap me across my face. "Don't you dare call me that. I'm not—"

"Marrying a man for money? Fucking a stranger for money? Don't kid yourself about what you will become if you do this."

My vision blurs through tears. I'm not a whore. I'm desperate. We're desperate. Why can't he see that this is our way out of this bitter hell.

"Go," he says, shoving me towards the door. "Go and marry your rich husband. Hopefully you won't disgust him the way you disgust me."

My heart shatters. And every broken piece of me withers. How can he say these things to me? How?

I can't be here. I can't be near him right now. I shove past him and grab for the door handle, scrambling for open space. For air.

"Alena..." His voice is pained and swollen behind me.

It's too late. It's too fucking late. He said those horrible things and now he can't take them back. The door slams against the wall and I fling myself out through the doorway.

"Alena. Wait!"

I aim for the stairwell. I can hear Dimitri trying to reassure our neighbours that everything is fine. Just a little misunderstanding.

A misunderstanding? The man I love thinks I'm a whore. I disgust him.

I'm sobbing and my breathing has gone hard and jagged as I run down the grey concrete stairs, my hand on the balustrade because I can barely see where I'm going.

"I'm serious, Alena. You stop right now." His voice echoes from above me.

I won't. I can't.

"If you leave...you...you can't fucking come back," he roars.

Fuck him. I won't come back. See how he likes it. I push the exit and stumble out into the street. Space. I need air. The wind is sharp against the rivers on my cheeks as I try to outrun my pain.

"Fine. Leave!" he screams after me as I sprint towards the dying sun, my legs numb as they carry me. "You'll be nothing without me. You hear me? *Nothing!*"

Chapter Ten

Dimitri

The second that Alena slips from my view, my fury drains from me.

What have I done?

I let the anger take over again. I let it bleed into my veins like a poison. I let it control me like a ghostly possession. She's still such a child, barely a woman. She didn't deserve it. But, God, the thought of some strange man touching her...

I know Alena, I *know* her. She wouldn't have considered Isabelle's offer if she didn't think it was the best thing for *us*. As much as I want to, I can't hate her for lying to me. I can't hate her for clawing onto Isabelle's glittering offer. I understand her desperation. I feel it too. I feel it curling in the pit of my stomach and poisoning my blood. I feel it late at night when she's asleep, the helplessness tearing through me so roughly I want to scream. Instead I grip my hands into fists and make bloody crescents in my palms. Then I get up the next morning and try a little harder, even though it gets a little harder to try every day.

I blame her father, the worthless piece of shit who didn't even stick around long enough for her to be born. For making her fear deep down that all men are destined to leave her. For making her desperate for a Plan B of her own. If he had only gotten one look at her sweet, innocent face, one touch of her soft, generous hands, one glimpse of her dreamer's heart, he would have fallen in love with her like I had.

I blame her mother for never being there for her. For abandoning her when it got too hard. For making her crave the approval of an older woman, a motherly figure she can look up to. Isabelle is preying on that. Isabelle is preying on *her*. She's just fifteen, for fuck's sake.

Mostly, I blame myself. If only I could take care of my lamb properly. If only I could give her everything she needed, everything she wanted, everything she dreamed.

I understand, Alena. We're on a cliff. I'm the one you're hanging on to. But I'm hanging on by my fingers. I have to keep us from falling but I keep slipping no matter what I do.

I'm trying, Alena. But it's not good enough. Inadequacy slices me from the inside, letting my failures dribble out.

She thinks that signing up with the GW Agency means that she can be the one to pull us up. But at what cost?

The horrible words I hurdled at her come back to punch me in the gut and the air whooshes out of me. You stupid man. You could lose her. You may have already lost her. The thought stabs my heart and twists. I gasp from the pain.

I can't lose her.

I can't.

I run after her.

Chapter Eleven

Alena

The present...

I'm roused from sleep by the sound of tyres crunching over gravel. Ghostly light peers through my curtains, so I know it's early, the morning chill seeping through my partly open window. Too early. In a half-dream state, I wonder who has arrived.

I snap up to sitting as a realisation dawns on me. I fling my bedcovers off and run to the window. I catch a glimpse of a familiar figure in a black overcoat sliding out of the Bentley below. Shit. My husband's home. He wasn't supposed to be here until later this morning. I must speak to him before Mrs Bates does. I grab the dressing gown hanging over one of my chairs and rush out of my room, wrapping it around me as I run down the corridor. He'll hate that I'm not dressed properly, but it'll be even worse if he hears about my miscarriage from her. My lower belly still cramps a bit, but I ignore it as I sprint through the corridor, my breath growing heavy.

I race down the stairs, the cold marble biting at my bare feet. Midway down, the stark, cavernous foyer comes into view. I come to a halt.

There is my husband. Mrs Bates huddled at his side like a conspirator.

I am too late.

My husband looks up and catches my eye, his brows drawing over his strong nose, his deep-set eyes turning dark, his thin lips pinching. He lifts a finger and curls it slowly, once, ordering me to come.

My heart hammers in my chest as I descend. Mrs Bates has added a smug look to her usual scowl.

"That'll be all, Mrs Bates," my husband says.

I can feel the disappointment rolling off her. She wanted to bear witness to my punishment. Bitch.

She bobs her head. "Of course, Mr Worthington." She shoots one last smug look at me before she leaves the foyer.

I barely notice. My feet are unsteady as I approach him. He says nothing, merely turns on his heel and marches into the small room to the side of the foyer, a wood panelled den he often uses to entertain male guests.

I follow him into the room.

"Close the door."

I do. I take a deep breath and turn around to face him once more. "Edgar—"

"Five years," he spits out. "Five years and you still haven't delivered me an heir."

"I'm sorry." Unwanted tears begin to roll down my cheeks. I swipe at them, begging them to stop. He hates it when I cry.

"You're sorry? You lose *another* baby and all you can say is *I'm sorry*?" He shoves me back, hard. I bang my head against the door.

Before I can move his palm lashes out, striking me on my cheek with a crack. Pain explodes across my face. I can't help the cry that rips from me. If only I had gotten to him earlier, perhaps I could have framed it in a way that I could have avoided his anger.

I hear him sigh. His face screws up before it partly disappears behind the hand he uses to rub his forehead. "Get out." His voice is hollow.

I don't hesitate. I flee from the den and run to my room, where I slam the door behind me and burrow deep into my blankets. Only then do I let the tears come freely.

What I wouldn't give to disappear far, far away.

I have no money, no friends except for Emily. I wouldn't get five miles before he found me and hauled me back. I know, because I tried that once during the first year I was here. I was punished for that too.

As always when I start to fall apart, Dimitri appears in my mind. He smiles at me, the way he used to, touches my cheek. *"You can do anything, Alena."* Even when he's no longer physically here, he's here for me. I nurse this tiny flame of hope inside me. I can't let it go out. If it goes out, I'm as good as dead.

I will have a baby. I will get the money owed to me. When I do, I will take my child and Emily, if she wants—I can't leave her here alone. She is as much a prisoner as I am—and we'll run away together across the sea. To America. To find the man who still holds my heart and beg his forgiveness.

My husband might have my body, but he'll never have my heart or my soul. Those I gave to one man a long time ago.

Chapter Twelve

Dimitri

Five years ago...

I turn the corner Alena disappeared around. I can't see her. I spin, searching the streets that branch off for a sign of where she's gone. She has a few friends at school, but she's not close enough to any of them to turn to them. I am the only one she has. Except...

I run—like my life is at stake—back to Isabelle's agency.

I approach the dark door for a second time in...has it been less than an hour since I was here? Since I carried Alena out, fighting and screaming? No one is around. I can't spot anyone at the windows, curtains drawn. I eye the silent door that seems to stare back and weigh my options. There's no way anyone is letting me in for a second time. They'll likely call the police if I bang on the door again. They won't let me in. I just need to talk to her, to hold her, to tell her I'm sorry—then everything will be okay.

Perhaps there is another entrance or even an open window. I slip along the building until I find a slim gate. Through it I can see a passage between the buildings. I spy what looks like a courtyard beyond. The courtyard, of course. A lot of these old buildings are built around one. The gate is unlocked, thank God. It squeaks as I push it open enough to squeeze my frame through, my feet almost silent on the cobblestones. I hear voices as I near the end of the passageway.

"…doesn't understand."

I suck in a breath. That's Alena. The sound of pain in her voice cuts me. I can't bear to hear her cry. *I'm sorry, my love. I'm sorry.* I'm about to step out when she says something that makes me freeze.

"I hate Dimitri," she hisses. "He's selfish and cruel. And his temper… You should have heard all the insults he hurled at me."

My blood curdles with guilt. *If I could take back every word, Alena.*

"He's nothing but a thief and a simpleton. He's never going to be anything more."

My stomach stabs with the spearheads of all my failings, brought to life with her words.

Nothing but a thief.

A simpleton.

Never going to be anything more.

Deep down I think all these things. Deep down I fear they are true. But I never suspected that she thought this.

"It would *kill* me to marry Dimitri. I have to accept the Englishman. God, what I wouldn't give to leave this horrible place. What I wouldn't give to have a better life."

She can't mean that. I clutch at the brick wall, the passageway closing in on me, my vision blurring. I can't breathe. I need air. Air. I need.

"If Dimitri can't see that…he can stay here in hell and rot, see if I care."

Her words are the forged steel of a sword slicing me right through my heart.

Here it is. The truth of what she believes of me. The truth she had never dared to say to my face. All this time…I thought she loved me. She is everything to me. I thought she felt the same. Turns out I am just another love-sick fool so easily tossed aside when a better offer comes along.

"Don't marry him, marry me. I don't have a ring now but I will get one. I will. I can give you everything you've ever wanted. I promise, just…"

She tugs her hand from mine, the loss of it spreading a frost through me like sickness. *"Get up. You look ridiculous on the floor."*

I can't hear anymore.

I can't.

I stumble back, back through the passageway, tripping over my own feet, tumbling through the gate. When I hit the pavement, I begin to run. I am numb, wrapped in fuzzy cotton. I can barely feel my feet. But I sense the bubbling roar of anguish chasing after me like a tsunami. When it hits me…God help me.

I fear I can't outrun it for long.

Chapter Thirteen

Alena

"I have to accept the Englishman," I say to Natassia, the GW's dark-haired receptionist. Even as I say these words, my voice sounds hollow. I squeeze my eyes shut, but every time I do, I see Dimitri on his knees in front of me. I remember my cold words to him and they spear me through my heart. I snap my eyes open and focus on Natassia's face, her lovely features drawn into a look of concern.

She and I are sitting on a wrought-iron bench in the courtyard of Isabelle's agency, so the girls inside can't hear us. She is the only one here who knows the truth about Dimitri. That he's not my brother. She's promised not to tell. I don't trust her, exactly. I don't know her. But I had to talk to *someone*. I just have to hope that she keeps her word.

"What I wouldn't give to leave this horrible place," I spit out. "What I wouldn't give to have a better life." I just want to know what it's like to be warm and fed and happy. I want to know what it means not to have to worry all the time. Is that too much to ask for? Bitter frustration bubbles up within my well of hurt. "If Dimitri can't see that…he can stay here and rot, see if I care."

A sharp wind blows and the creak of the front gate sounds out of the passageway. Natassia slides a hand on my shoulder. She has been so kind to me since I first came here. "If that's how you truly feel, then go and make your slice of Heaven with the Englishman."

I remember Dimitri's face as he called me a whore. He will never agree to this arrangement. I know him—once he forms an opinion, he won't let it go. My chest wells up with such a sharp emotion that I stop breathing for a second. "Why does Heaven seem to cost so much?" I ask, barely a whisper.

It costs me…Dimitri.

I have to give him up.

The thought slashes through me, a lightning strike trying to cleave my soul in two. It illuminates our past, our history, the very intertwining weave of our two lives. There's no joy that Dimitri and I both don't share. No pain that we don't live through together. A realisation strikes me with such force I double over, sucking in air.

Dimitri and I are two parts of one soul.

He *is* my soul.

How can a full belly be satisfying if my soul is left hungry? How can I truly be warm if my heart is left cold?

What sapphires could please me more than Dimitri's eyes? What symphony as rich as his laughter? What finest silk could compare to being wrapped up in his arms? All the world could crumble and wither into ash, but if he were still alive, I'd still be happy.

Suddenly the rain and mist inside me clears. Everything is clear and fresh, like the first day of spring.

I look up from my hands, twisted together in my lap. Natassia is frowning at me, asking if I'm okay.

"Oh, Natassia," I breathe, "I've been such a fool." My blood rushes with purpose, my veins swollen with clarity. "I need to find Dimitri." I fling myself from my seat and begin to run, my soul feeling like it has remembered its wings, now taking flight.

I burst into our apartment, eyes seeking the man I love more than life itself, his sacred name on my lips. I blink rapidly, hardly able to believe what I'm seeing. The place has been ruined, furniture dashed to splintered pieces, our vinyl record in shards, scattered fallen pages all that remain of my books. Through the smashed windows, a bitter wind blows in, making me shiver.

I can almost see Dimitri as he stumbled back into the apartment after our fight—what set him off? What did he see that broke the dam of his rage? I can feel him falling apart, his tormented pain still hovering like a ghost, clinging to each shattered item.

"If you leave...you...you can't fucking come back," he roars.

He thought I was never coming back. My heart jams up into my throat, choking me.

I did this.

I destroyed him.

"No," releases from my lips in a whisper. My knees give out. I sink to the floor, my fingers clawing at the carpet.

They catch on a shredded piece of bright white lace that I don't recognise as being mine. I see the shredded box, the wrapping paper. I realise instantly that this was supposed to have been for me. For my sixteenth birthday. In two days.

In seeking Heaven, I reached too far. I flew too high with wings made of wax. Now I've fallen.

I have ruined us both.

Chapter Fourteen

Alena

The present…

At Worthington Manor, dinner is served at eight o'clock every night in the grand dining room. A monstrous wooden table that can seat twenty-four people plus elbow room is the main feature in this high-ceilinged room, original woodwork panels mixed with deep green wallpaper, glass cabinets and serving tables; at each end is a grand fireplace so large I can stand in it. I sit opposite Emily and we wait, hands in laps, for my husband to honour us with his presence at the place at the head of the table between us.

"Did you tell him?" she asks, a slight crease between her brows. I know she's talking about my miscarriage.

I glance over to the side of the dining room. There's only a young maid waiting there to serve us. I know she won't tell on us. I turn back to Emily. "Mrs Bates had that pleasure."

At the mention of Mrs Bates, Emily makes a face like she's tasted something awful. Then her features turn piteous. "Poor Papa," Emily says. "He must be so sad."

I wince slightly as I remember her father's anger earlier. Thankfully Emily hasn't noticed. She's watching the door for her father. She would die if she knew what was going on under her nose. She doesn't know I was bought. She doesn't know that her father only keeps me as a brood mare to deliver him a son. I will never tell her.

"And you..." Emily turns towards me. "How are you?"

If she wasn't so damn sweet, I'd hate her for being his daughter. But I know she's practically a prisoner here too. *The world is a wild and terrible place*, he said. *It's my duty to protect you from it.* She was homeschooled growing up. Now that she's finished school, I'm certain that my dear husband will come home one day with a husband for her. And she'll accept it. Despite his coldness towards her, she has this desperate need to please him.

Speak of the devil...

My husband enters the dining room and takes his seat, no apology for keeping us waiting. Thank God. I'm starving. The smell of the roast chicken and baked potatoes has been torturing me. I pick up my knife and fork. For a few minutes, the air fills with the sound of knives scraping plates and of chewing.

"I've invited a Mr Wolf to stay with us next week," my husband says between large bites of food. "You're both to make him feel welcome."

I force down the bite of food in my mouth. The men my husband associates with are as bad as he is. My husband's friends leave Emily alone because she's his daughter. They know who I am and exactly how much my husband paid for me. They treat me as such.

I've never heard him speak of Mr Wolf before. I want to ask but Emily beats me to it. "Who is Mr Wolf?"

"He's an investor here from America. I met him in London. He's looking for a business to invest in. I'm hoping it'll be mine." My husband operates a finance company specialising in shares management. He didn't share the details with me. I had to look them up.

"What's he like?" Emily's face is alert and her eyes sparkling with possibilities. "Is he young?"

My husband shrugs and helps himself to more potatoes. "Mid-twenties, I'd say. Tall fellow. Has a foreign accent so I don't think he's originally from America. Although his English is very good."

Emily is smiling with her chin resting on her hand. I know in her head she's half in love with Mr Wolf already. You can hardly blame her. She's an eighteen-year-old girl who has never been kissed, who is barely let out of this gilded cage. I hope he's not handsome enough to break her heart. I ignore the twinge of nerves over Mr Wolf's upcoming arrival.

I'm still feeling weak from my miscarriage, so I'm the first to leave dinner. My slippered feet barely make a sound on the marble floor as I pass into the main foyer.

I flinch as I take in the figure of the man who's standing just inside the entrance, brushing the collar and shoulders of his coat from the English drizzle. Terrance Hagerty, my husband's business advisor, a man in his mid-forties with a rat-like face and spidery hands. I gulp back a gasp. Of all my husband's associates, I hate him the most. My skin breaks out into goose bumps.

I don't want him to see me. Maybe if I back up slowly into the shadows—

As if he has heard me, he looks up, his beady grey eyes locking on mine. A smile crawls across his face. "Alena." His voice is nasally and barbed. "How lovely to see you again."

I wish I could say the same for you.

I force my features into an expression of placid politeness and nod my head in greeting. "My husband is still in the dining room. Excuse me. I'm not feeling well." I start for the staircase, my movements jerky in my haste to get away from him.

His fingers close around my arm before I can escape, my skin crawling at his touch.

"Come now, Alena." His sour breath curdles around my cheeks. "Are you really going to run away so quickly? We really must catch up." He smiles and reveals a set of yellowing teeth.

I tug against him. His grip tightens so hard that I wince. I see the flare of pleasure in his eyes.

"Let go of me or I will scream," I hiss.

"Alena?" A soft feminine voice startles us both.

Emily is standing at the corridor from the dining room. She's staring at his hand wrapped around my arm.

With his plans thwarted, Terrance lets go of me and takes a step back. I clutch my red wrist to my chest. He smiles at her, but it's poisonous underneath the surface. "Lovely Emily. Alena and I were just…catching up."

Emily hurries to my side and slings her arm through mine. "Father's expecting you. He's gone into the drawing room. You shouldn't keep him waiting." She drags me up the stairs.

"Thank you," I whisper to her.

"He's so fucking creepy," she whispers back. "Sleep in my room tonight?"

I nod with relief. Terrance often stays here the night if he and my husband have business together. I'm not sure whether he'd ever "accidentally" find himself in my room in the middle of the night, but I don't want to find out.

"Good night, Mr Haggard," Emily calls back down the stairs, deliberately saying his name wrong.

I muffle a giggle. God, I love her.

I can feel his eyes burning into my back. When I chance a glance back, Terrance is standing at the base of the stairs, watching us leave. He has a look on his face that says: *One day. I'll get you alone. One day soon.*

Chapter Fifteen

Alena

Five years ago...

The cream lace dress I wear is flawless. It's the girl inside that is torn. My palms are sweaty as I press them to my stomach, trying to hold my pieces in. Edgar Worthington, my soon-to-be husband looks down at me out of the corner of his eye as we stand in front of the celebrant at St Petersburg City Hall. He is not as tall as Dimitri but tall enough that I have to look up at him. I see grey eyes and a soft, thin-lipped smile before his face blurs in my vision.

This feels wrong. It is wrong. But what choice do I have?

After I picked myself up off the floor of our ruined apartment, I ran to the factory where Dimitri worked. *He's quit*, they said, *gone to America*, they said. I spent the last of my money on a taxi to the airport. I raced up and down the terminal screaming his name until two security guards came and dragged me to a back office. Through my tears I explained my situation, I begged for their help. They went away and then, after what felt like an eternity, they came back with a piece of paper. A passenger's list. Dimitri Volkov was on a plane to New York, left twenty-three minutes ago. He was gone. I had lost him.

With winter coming, no place to live and no money to support me, I had no choice.

Marry this stranger or die.

I don't want to die. It would be easier if I did. My heart may be shattered, but my cursed survival instincts are still functioning. They're overriding everything else for now. Even the coiling instinct to *run!*

Isabelle is guarding my other side. As always, she is impeccably dressed in a powder blue pantsuit, her white mink coat flung over one gloved arm, large pearls around her neck. Natassia kept her word and said nothing to Isabelle about Dimitri. Isabelle smiles sweetly at me, but I can see the truth in her eyes. She is here to ensure the wedding goes through and the contracts are signed. She is here to protect her investment.

I barely remember hearing the vows or the translator repeating in English what the priest says in Russian. I don't remember saying "I do." But I must have. Because suddenly I'm bending over and my fingers are trembling as I sign the marriage contract. My pen makes black loops around me, tying me up nice and tight, my signature right in between my husband's and Isabelle's.

My only way out is to produce a child. A bitter foreign seed sprouts in my gut, the poison tips breaking through the numbness. Before I can grab the contract and tear it to pieces, it is snatched from me. Isabelle slips it into a slim briefcase and hands it to one of her bodyguards, her lips pursed with satisfaction. I open my mouth to scream. Nothing comes out.

Marry him or die.

Another piece of paper is thrust in front of me. Someone stabs a black line with their finger. The marriage license. They want me to sign the marriage license now.

With a final slash of my pen, leaving a trail of bleeding black ink, I kill Alena Ivanova.

Standing in her place is a woman I don't know.

Mrs Edgar Worthington.

I will mourn Alena Ivanova. Soon. But not now. Not right now.

Under the numbness shrouding me is the pain howling underneath, sharpening its claws. It's waiting for me. It's coming.

Marry him or die.

I blink and Isabelle is hugging me, her expensive perfume like a gas clogging up my nostrils and my eyes. "Congratulations, Alena," she says in her accented Russian. "I'm so happy for you." Her words bounce right off me. Then she's striding away, her bodyguards trailing after her like two giant Dobermans. Leaving me in the hands of a stranger.

I feel a firm hand grip my elbow. It's my husband. He's frowning at me. Oh, right. The ceremony is over.

I am married.

Married.

The word echoes inside my body as if I am an empty cavern.

I also turn sixteen today. But nobody mentions that.

My new husband drapes a thick fur coat over my shoulders. It's real. I can smell the hint of earthy wildness in the fur. My Jimmy Choo heels clack against the marble as he leads me to a limousine waiting outside. I've never been in one before. Through the flakes of snow stinging my eyes, I see the driver holding the back door open for me. I stumble as I get into the heated vehicle. Right into the black leather seats. My new husband shoots me a smile and pats my knee, then we drive in silence. I know nothing about my new husband—God, that word sounds strange to me—except he is English. And he's older than me.

The limo stops in front of the Belmond Grand Hotel, an imposing building with rows of tall casement windows guarded by stone statues. Within minutes, we've checked in and we're being escorted up to the Presidential Suite by the manager himself, a slim, polished man who speaks to my husband in proud, accented English, his hands as graceful as a conductor as he points out this and that. We are trailed by porters who carry my husband's luggage and our coats.

On the top floor, the manager holds open the door to the penthouse suite and sneers at me behind my husband's back. I don't have the heart to tell him that his shallow judgements are specks of shit on the ass of a flea in the spectrum of things I give a fuck about right now. I walk into the suite after my husband and halt right inside.

This place is a palace. I'm standing in the living room, crystal chandeliers glinting off gold and coral wallpaper, clusters of red velvet armchairs, a bucket of champagne and two flutes sitting on the low cherry wood table. Like the rest of this hotel, it's heated enough not to need a coat. This room alone is twice the size of the studio I shared with Dimitri—thinking his name sends a stab of something white-hot through my numbness. This room probably costs more per night than I've ever seen in my life. There are more rooms showing through open doors, a closed glass wrap-around terrace showing through thick gold curtains held aside with wide ties. The snow is falling harder now, the flakes beating at the glass.

Here I am in a penthouse suite. Let's toast with champagne to my charmed life.

The door clicks behind me like the cocking of a pistol. I suddenly realise that I am alone here with my husband. The manager's gone. So are the porters. Just him and me.

This time his hand rests on my lower back—too low—as he leads me through one of the doors. To the bedroom, another spacious, opulent room. Anxiousness ties another knot in my stomach. The bed looks monstrous enough to swallow me whole.

He unzips my dress from behind. The material peels off me down to the plush carpet. In seconds my strapless bra and panties are stripped off me too.

I am naked.

Naked.

I've never been naked in front of anyone before.

Dimi was supposed to be the one undressing me today. I was supposed to be wearing white lace instead of cream.

My husband walks around me, inspecting me as if I were a steed that he just bought at a market. I suppose I am. I think he likes what he sees because he smiles and mumbles something, his fingers exploring my breasts and down the quivering plane of my stomach. His touch is foreign. Removed.

Still, my nipples harden when he rubs and tweaks them. This single reaction of my body feels like a betrayal. Not just to Dimitri. But to me.

He fashions me into position like a doll, kneeling on all fours on the mattress that sinks like quicksand. I stare at the painting behind the bed of a ship on the horizon and wish I were on it, wherever it was going. My fingers grip the sheets as I hear the tinkling of his belt coming undone. Dread coagulates in the pit of my stomach, making me feel ill. I feel his fingers on my hips, his erection between my legs and I shut my eyes.

I hiss as he invades my body, a sharp pain cutting through my numb shield. He smells all wrong, like tobacco and a woodsy perfume that tickles my nose. He starts to move. With every thrust of his I chant.

I hate you, Dimitri.
Fuck you for leaving me.
I hate you.
I hate you.
I love you.

My husband jerks behind me. He comes with a moan, calling out what sounds like another woman's name. When he pulls out, relief floods me like warm liquid. No, it *is* warm liquid, running down the inside of my thigh. I stumble to the en suite, a museum of marble and mirrors, and clean myself up, taking my time. There is it, stark red on white tissue, the remnants of my innocence. I look up and catch my reflection in one of the full-length mirrors. I don't recognise the girl I see. My cheeks burn. I find the robe behind the door and cover my body up.

When I return to the bedroom, my new husband is lying across the sheets, mopping the sweat pouring from his forehead with a handkerchief. He asks me something in English.

I shake my head. "Sorry," I say in my heavily accented English.

He points at me and yells, "Brother? Brother?"

It takes me a moment to recognise this English word. He is asking about Dimitri. Where is Dimitri?

My numbness grows brittle. It starts to crack. The tears seep out before I can stop them.

My husband makes no movement to comfort me. He merely frowns at me.

In the back of my mind, I realise that my tears are annoying him. I can't annoy my husband so soon after we're married. He's all I have now.

I gather all my childish feelings like scattered toys and place them into a box in my mind. I am a woman now. A married woman. I have no room for these things anymore.

I wipe my face and try for a smile. "I sorry," I say in an attempt at English. It's a language I will have to learn. I doubt my husband will learn Russian for me. Besides, Isabelle told me we'd be living in England after our short honeymoon here in St Petersburg.

"Brother?" my husband asks once more.

Dimitri's face appears in my mind again.

Dimitri left. I am all I have.

I shake my head, my lips pinched. "Brother dead."

Chapter Sixteen

Alena

The present…

It's late afternoon and Emily, my husband and I are standing in a row in the foyer waiting for the venerable Mr Wolf. Standing opposite us are Terrance and Mrs Bates. It feels so formal I almost want to burp, just to break the tension. It's like we're about to receive the queen. My husband demanded that we make ourselves presentable, i.e. uncomfortable. He keeps tugging on the sleeves of his tailored black suit and fixing his navy-blue tie. Emily looks sweet in a pale pink chiffon spaghetti-strap evening dress that falls to her knees, her hair pulled up into a French twist, showcasing her slender pale neck.

I'm dressed in a couture champagne-coloured dress that fits like a glove, feathers and beads dressing the skirt of the dress, made specifically for me by Vivienne Westwood, a present from my husband. He's always sorry after he lashes out at me. But he only says it with diamonds or couture. On my feet are a pair of Jimmy Choos, a stylish stiletto in a nude colour. My usually wild hair has been styled straight as a waterfall, cascading down over one of my smoky eyes and bright red lipstick.

My husband demanded that I wear the most expensive pieces of jewellery, so dripping from my ears are a pair of vintage chandelier diamond earrings. Around my neck is a heavy centrepiece necklace of white and yellow diamonds. It's almost like a collar, and the gold and diamond links drip down between my breasts. My husband thinks I look fit to stand beside him. I think I look like one of those stars you place on top of the Christmas tree. Funny how I used to dream of wearing things like this. Now I would trade it all to have Dimitri back.

Through the frosted glass in our entrance doors, I spot a car pulling up into our circular driveway, gravel crushing underneath the tyres.

My husband stiffens at my side, then hisses down to me. "I'm sure I don't have to tell you that this investor is very, very important to us."

"I know," I say quietly.

"Charm him. You have a way. Make him feel welcome. Make him feel at home. Whatever he wants, he gets."

"Of course."

He straightens his tie once again, then leans in. "Whatever you do, *don't* fuck this up for me."

My blood curdles. If anything goes wrong on this investor's trip, I will be to blame. I have a feeling my punishment, should anything go wrong, will be worse than I've ever experienced.

I steady my nerves as a figure appears out of the black town car and walks up the steps to completely darken the width of the glass. My breath sucks into the back of my throat. He is huge. At least six feet two and his shoulders are wide as a rugby player.

The footman at the door clears his throat. "I present, Mr Wolf." He opens the front door with a flourish. Mr Wolf steps into our foyer, his long grey overcoat swishing at his ankles.

Oh. My. God.

My heart seizes. My lungs cramp. My world shatters into a million little pieces.

There standing before me is Dimitri Volkov.

He's Mr Wolf? The American investor? There must be some mistake.

Then it hits me. Volkov is Russian for Wolf.

Why hadn't I made the connection?

Because I never thought, not in a million years, that Dimitri would come here to find me.

Everything fades around him. He is all I see. He is all that exists. He was always handsome but now, as a man of twenty-four, he is devastating. His hair is combed back into a more conservative style, but I can see pieces of it attempting to escape, wanting to dance like a wild wind. His jaw has become wide, sterner, stronger. His beautiful cheekbones, even more sculpted. His boyish beauty has been honed into a sharp and savage masculinity.

The footman proceeds to take his overcoat from him as Dimitri's eyes scan the foyer with the polished ease of someone used to all this opulence. He is no longer lean from lack of food and being overworked. He is thick and built like a man who works out every day. His torso is wide and his legs are strong, filling out his gorgeous light grey pinstriped suit. That, along with the pale blue of his shirt and the silver of his tie, looks so much more sophisticated than my husband's self-conscious attire. Dimitri wears Armani as if he were born in it.

My head spins and I feel as if I am in a dream. Dimitri. Here.

My body tumbles with so many questions. Where have you been? How did you come here? What have you been doing for the last five years? I want to know every single detail of every single day. Where do you live? Who did you meet? Do you remember me?

And mostly, the question burning in my heart…do you still love me?

It's been five years. But my heart still beats for you.

Five years.

But how—*how*—is he here?

Is this a strange coincidence? Did he happen to come across my husband in London?

Or did Dimitri know who my husband was? Did he come here to see *me*? My insides surge with hope, my soul dusting off her wings once more. He's here for me. He's going to take me away from this awful place and we can go to America like he promised all those years ago. Oh, Dimitri. I knew you hadn't forgotten about me just like I haven't forgotten about you. You have to know that I forgive you for leaving me behind all those years ago. I don't care, because you're here now and all is forgiven. You came for me.

Finally his gaze comes to rest on me. It hits me like a sucker punch to the gut.

My lips part as I struggle to breathe. It gets worse as my mouth completely dries. My heart beats wildly in my chest like a tribal shaman's dance. My entire soul is vibrating for the first time in five years. I was dead, but now I am alive. I am whole again.

Oh my God, Dimitri. You have no idea how many times I dreamed of seeing you again. Every day I thought of you. Every night I prayed you were safe and happy.

I want to say all these things, but they jam up against my voice box and not even a squeak leaves me. Not even a gasp. I want to run to him, fling my arms around his neck and cover his face with kisses. But I am too rooted in the ground and too dizzy to move.

Chapter Seventeen

Dimitri

Five years I have waited. Five years I have planned.
Five years I have worked towards this moment.
Now I am treading the first steps down destiny's path. The path that *she* set me on all those years ago.
Revenge. A dish best served cold.
But as my eyes rest upon her, I don't expect to be smacked in the face with how she's changed. I didn't expect this savage surge of fiery hatred in my veins.
She is no longer a girl of fifteen. Her body has bloomed with womanly curves, being hugged and shown off by her dress, her stunning neckpiece falling between generously formed breasts. I try not to think of what she would look like under her clothes. Her hair is long and straight, falling

over her shoulders like a golden waterfall. Straight hair? I frown. I don't like it this way. Where have those wild curls gone?

Some things haven't changed. Like her eyes, still the same dappled green and yellow, like leaves when they start to turn. Now they're filled with shock and, there it is…the longing underneath. It feels like she sees right into me. The love in her eyes is like fingers prying open my heart again. A tumble of unwanted feelings that I thought I had crushed underneath my boot begin to rise like a phoenix out of the ashes. I shove them down.

Fuck her. Fuck her for gazing at me with such longing and desire in her eyes. Fuck her for looking the way she does.

I *do not* love her. I am not that stupid little boy anymore. She ripped out my heart and tore it to pieces all those years ago. I will not fall for her charms again. This is just…wisps of nostalgia threatening to derail me. I will not be derailed. I slam down the cold mask across my face and my soul. She will never get inside again. Never.

Her soft, supple mouth parts in a gasp and I force myself to remember all those brutal words that spilled from that pretty mouth all those years ago. I feel the wounds they made as if it were yesterday.

"He's nothing but a thief and a simpleton. He's never going to be anything more." I repeat her cursed words in my head, the words that revealed the truth of her cruel, shallow heart. *"It would kill me to marry Dimitri."*

My heart hardens, turning to ice. *Yes, good.* I remind myself of the *only* reason I am here.

Revenge.

If she still loves me then this will be icing on the cake to my plan. It will make her hurt all the more.

Bit by bit, she will watch her charmed life crumble to the ground.

Then, when she needs me the most, when she is desperate, scared and alone like I was all those years ago...

I will destroy her.

Chapter Eighteen

Alena

Dimitri is here. He is here.

My husband's voice greeting Dimitri breaks through my reverie.

Shit. I'm not alone with Dimi. Emily and my husband are here next to me. *My husband.*

Thankfully, my husband is so besotted with Mr Wolf that he doesn't notice my utter shock and the gale force of emotions tearing through me. My husband uses lavish words, his voice tighter than usual, his desperation to please is so thick, it's almost suffocating. This nags at me. My husband is never as flustered as this. He's never the one to need the approval of others. He must want Dimitri's investment badly. But why?

Dimitri's large hand practically swallows my husband's. I remember how those hands used to find the skin of my belly, the way he'd touch me with them, full of tenderness and fire. Heat coils in my lower belly.

Dimitri turns to me but Emily steps in our way. I feel a small stab and have to repress the urge to shove her aside.

"Oh, Mr Wolf," she gushes, her voice light and breathy, "we've heard so much about you. We're so happy you could come and stay." I can almost imagine how her eyelashes are fluttering, like that time she had a crush on the young gardener and wanted to spend all her time "enjoying the outdoors," even though it was in the middle of a freezing winter.

Oh God. Emily is developing a crush on Dimitri.

I can't blame her. Dimitri is utterly mesmerising. Still, a sickness starts to grow in my heart.

"I am very happy to be here, Miss Emily." Oh God, his voice. Dimitri's beautiful baritone has deepened even further. It reverberates through the air like a bass note in a slow blues number.

Finally, Dimitri steps around Emily and faces me. We are less than a metre away from each other. Longing rips through my ribcage. I shouldn't be staring but I can't tear my eyes away.

It's Dimi. My Dimi. He's here for me.

His deep-set piercing blue eyes used to simmer with heat and warmth as they looked back at me. Now as his gaze comes to rest upon me, they are as cold as ice. There's no warmth in his face. No surprise. No happiness. None. Like he doesn't know me. The only outward appearance of emotion is a slight narrowing of his eyes.

"Mrs Worthington," he says.

It sounds so formal I could cry. *Don't be like this, Dimi. It's me. It's Alena.*

"It's so lovely to meet you." He stretches out his hand.

How can I accept a mere handshake when my body is screaming to throw itself into him arms?

A realisation slaps me in the face. Of course. Dimitri can't act like he knows me. We need to keep our past a secret if we have any chance of leaving here together. My husband won't let go of me—his possession—so easily. His pride won't let him. *Oh, Dimi. I've waited for you for so long.*

I force a steady breath. "Likewise, Mr Wolf." I reach for him, my fingers trembling.

My hand slides into his.

Our first touch in five years.

A riot of fireworks whizz and flare up my arm and down my body. My breath catches. Emotions jam up in the back of my throat.

His eyes widen imperceptibly. For a second, a mere second, the ice in his features melt and I see the Dimitri I used to know looking back out at me.

Then his eyes freeze over again.

His hand is firm but smoother than they were, his old callouses almost unnoticeable. He hasn't worked with his hands in a long time.

"Your husband has told me much about you." He slides his other hand over mine, trapping me. "In terms of your beauty, he has not exaggerated. As for your other braggable qualities, they are yet to be discovered." His words are honey and lightness, but I can hear the bite in his voice. The way he spits out the word *husband.* The slight scorn when he mentions my undiscovered *braggable qualities.*

I part my lips in shock. I can't move as he tugs his hands from mine, my skin burning from where he touched me. Could he still be angry with me? After all these years?

I want to search his face again. But he has turned away already, back to my husband. I catch the eye of Mr Haggerty, staring at me with narrowed eyes.

I snap my mouth shut. He can't find out about Dimitri and me. No one can. I school my features as best as I can and try to keep my mind from spinning.

"I hope you don't mind, I have my business advisor arriving soon," Dimitri says.

"Certainly not," my husband says after a slight pause. "We'll have the guest room next to you made up for him."

"Thank you."

"Emily," my husband says, "please check with cook that everything is ready for dinner. Alena can show Mr Wolf to his room."

"But Papa, I thought I could show Mr—"

"And have Alena oversee our dinner?" He lets out a curt, cruel laugh at my expense. "I'd rather not have burned food. Neither would our guest. Alena doesn't know the first useful thing about running a kitchen."

I stiffen. "We can't all have Emily's domestic abilities."

My husband's hard eyes are focused on me. "Yes, but I would settle for at least *one* ability."

My cheeks flame. He's still angry at me over the loss of our baby. *It's not my fault,* I want to scream. *I wanted him too. More than you.*

I catch Dimitri's gaze and I see no empathy. Just an empty coldness in his eyes. He turns to my husband. "Your footman can show me to my room. I'm sure Mrs Worthington has more important wifely duties to perform."

"Nonsense," my husband says with a laugh. "My wife has nothing better to do."

Nothing better to do. That's me. A kept woman. Useless except for showing guests to their room.

I lift my head high. "Please follow me, Mr Wolf. I'll have one of the footmen bring up your luggage later."

Chapter Nineteen

Alena

I can feel Dimitri's eyes on my back as he follows me up the stairs. My heart tumbles around my chest as we disappear from sight of the others and make our way through the corridors. Each one of his footsteps, echoing over mine, makes my insides flinch. My ankles and knees feel like they're being held together by loose bolts. I curse these heels. It takes everything in me not to stumble. To just focus on the next step.

We say nothing, the whole way. My head has never been filled with so many questions.

Where have you been? How did you get here? How did you find me?

The air around us has never been so thick with words.
I missed you. I'm sorry. I love you. I always will.

We reach the guest room in the west wing on the top floor, the one my husband instructed that he occupy. I push open the navy-painted door and step aside.

He steps right up to me, his nearness causing my body to heat and my head to go lightheaded. "Please," his eyes bore into mine, "after you."

He wants me to come inside his room?

Of course. We'll be alone inside. At last. We can talk. After five years I will get to say everything I have been longing to say. They all cram up into my throat. I swallow down a knot of anticipation and step into the room.

It's a glorious large room with high ceilings, king-sized bed, the décor styled in a rich navy and gold. A grey light streams in through the floor-to-ceiling windows that span across the outer wall.

The door slams shut behind us like a gunshot and I flinch.

Dimitri and I are alone.

Alone.

His presence is like a fire on my back. I need relief and yet, I yearn for him to move closer. The floor creaks as he takes a step towards me. My body explodes into shivers.

"This is the best guest room in the house," I ramble, my hands gripping the front of my dress to stop them from shaking. "It has a beautiful south-facing terrace overlooking the manicured back gardens and the moors on our estate. It gets quite a lot of sun. Well, for England."

"Stop pretending, Alena. I know you remember me."

I spin. The sight of him standing so close before me makes my heart beat a riot in my chest. "Oh, Dimi," I breathe and move towards him.

He holds up a hand, his lips lifting in a sneer. "I remember *you*."

I halt as his harsh tone lashes through me. My mind tries to wrap around this development. Why is he speaking like that? "Dimi?"

"Don't call me that. I am Mr Wolf to you."

My blood drains in my limbs. There is no need for pretences now that we're alone. This is his true self, his real feelings. He's never forgiven me for our fight all those years ago. My piecemeal heart breaks all over again. "You... You can't mean that."

"Why, Alena," he steps forward, closing the gap between us, "do my *words* hurt you?"

I hate that despite how cruelly he glares at me, I still want to hold him. I want to brush the scorn off his face, to rub my hands over his cold heart and bring it back to life.

"Why are you doing this? Why are you here?"

He leans in. His hot, sweet breath caressing my cheeks. "Why do you think?"

I shake my head, trying to clear my mind from the fog that descends over me with his nearness. "You want to hear how sorry I am? You want—?"

"I want a lot of things. None of which you deserve to be privy to anymore." He leans in. "Let me give you a hint. I'm not here for a soppy heartfelt reunion."

I can't believe this. *What's happened to you, Dimitri?* "You can't possibly still feel—"

"You don't get to tell me what I can or can't feel, *Mrs* Worthington." The way he says my married title is so full of bitterness.

"Don't fucking touch me, you whore."

His words slap me across my face. "Don't you dare call me that. I'm not—"

"Marrying a man for money? Fucking a stranger for money? Don't kid yourself at what you will become if you do this."

My vision blurs through tears. I'm not a whore. I'm desperate. We're desperate. Why can't he see that this is our way out of this bitter hell.

"Go," he says, shoving me towards the door. "Go and marry your rich husband. Hopefully you won't disgust him the way you disgust me."

I grit my teeth. He thinks I'm a whore. "It wasn't my fault that—"

"I don't want to hear your pathetic excuses. You said all I needed to hear all those years ago."

I'm not the only one who made mistakes. *He* was the one who left *me*. He is so stubborn that he will never admit his faults. So blinded with rage even after five years. Something snaps in me. "You stupid man. You're so full of bitterness, you wouldn't hear me if I tried to explain."

He snorts. "You're the stupid one. If only you had stuck with me, Alena. If only you just had faith. I could have given you all of this and more." He strides to the door and holds it open for me, cutting through our conversation. "Thank you for showing me to my room, Mrs Worthington." And we're back to formalities again.

I straighten, pride lifting my chin.

"I hope you enjoy your *short* stay, Mr Wolf," I say as I sweep past him.

"I'm sure I will."

Chapter Twenty

Alena

The door slams behind me. I make it two steps before I sag against the wall, fury bleeding out of me.

What the hell just happened?

This is Dimitri. He appeared after all this time and... I shouldn't have gotten so furious at him. But he was being so cold it was like chips of ice splintering into my skin.

I should go back and—

No. I will not bend before him. I will not beg for him.

His pride will not let him listen. Not yet. He just needs a few days here near me for him to soften. I know Dimitri. He could never stay angry at me. I just have to bear his anger, and wait.

I flinch as I take in the figure of the man who has just stepped into the corridor from the staircase, blocking my exit. Terrance's beady grey eyes lock on mine as he strides towards me. I straighten and school my features into what I hope is a semblance of calm.

"Alena, are you still feeling weak from your miscarriage?" His voice is pretty with concern, but I know it's fake.

Mrs Bates must have told him. Or my husband. I force a smile. "I'm fine, thank you."

"Your third one in a number of years. I wonder what you're doing wrong."

I brush off the barb. "Can I help you?"

His lip pinches and I know he's annoyed that I didn't bite at his veiled insult. "Is our guest settled?"

"Yes, of course."

He stops right before me, blocking my path. I realise too late that suspicion clouds his eyes. "And how do you know Mr Wolf?"

I try not to flinch. "I don't. I just met him today."

"Really?" His voice doesn't sound convinced at all. "Funny, you looked at him as if you recognised him."

"How strange. Perhaps he looks like someone I used to know." I brush off his interrogation. "Excuse me. I need to see about the other guest room."

He pushes me against the wall, blocking me with his body, his nearness making the bile rise into my throat. "Sweet, sweet Alena," his voice weasels into my ear. "You'll tell me the truth now, won't you?"

I push against him but he won't move. "Get away from me," I demand, trying to keep the fear out of my voice.

"What's going on here?" a stern voice demands. Dimitri's voice washes over me and I sag with relief.

Terrance lets go of me and steps away from me. I turn

and see my saviour standing just outside his doorway, his face like thunder.

"Mr Wolf," Terrance says, a smarmy smile on his face. He shakes the greasy hair out of his face. "I was just coming up to see how you were settling in."

"It looks like you were harassing Mrs Worthington."

Terrance lets out an awkward laugh. "Of course not."

Dimitri doesn't look convinced at all. He strides up to us, his dominating presence taking up most of the corridor. Terrance seems to withdraw into himself. I want to fling myself into Dimitri's arms—*see, you do still care*—but I restrain myself. "There is a special place in hell for men who force themselves on unwilling women."

"I wasn't—"

"Off you go, Alena." Dimitri's eyes burn into mine, demanding no argument. Power radiates off him, thick and coiled aggression. It makes my knees weak. I give him a nod, my breath coming out in short bursts.

I can feel Terrance scowling at me, but there's nothing he can do. I turn and hurry away.

"Where are my suitcases?" I hear Dimitri demand at Terrance behind me.

"Well, I—"

"Go and bring them to me."

"But..." Terrance splutters. "I'm not a footman."

"I don't damn well care. Go. Now!"

A thunder of footsteps comes up behind me. I press aside against the closest wall as Terrence flies past me like the devil is on his heels. I stifle a giggle. Then stiffen when I sense eyes on my back, hot like the sun.

I turn to look at Dimitri over my shoulder. He's already looking at me. My breath catches. My stomach warms. For a moment we just stare at each other, the air hanging heavy.

I find tears pricking at the backs of my eyes. God, I've missed him. I suck in a breath to compose myself. *Thank you,* I mouth.

I swear I see the subtle nod of his head before he turns away.

Chapter Twenty-One

Alena

Emily, my husband and I sit in the dining room. My husband is at the head of the table and I sit on his right. The spare place opposite me, between my husband and Emily, has been reserved for Dimitri, who has not yet arrived.

I clear my throat. "I thought, er, Terrance would be eating with us," I say casually. When he's here he usually joins us for dinner.

"No," my husband says, "he decided to return to London early."

I stifle a smile. I wouldn't be surprised if Dimitri had something to do with that. "So soon? How unfortunate for all of us." My sarcasm is lost on Edgar as it always is. I glance over to Emily to catch her eye and wink.

But she's not looking at me. She hasn't even heard me from the looks of it. She's got her head turned, watching the doorway. She's practically vibrating in her chair. "Where's Mr Wolf?"

"I'm sure he's coming," I say with more bite than I intended.

"Do you think I should go up to his room and see if everything's okay?"

My stomach stabs. *Leave him alone*, I want to yell. But I don't.

I clear my throat. "I'm sure he's fine."

"What if he's lost? This is such a big house."

Before Emily can jump out of her chair, Dimitri appears. He's changed out of his travelling suit. He wears a pressed pair of light grey slacks that showcase his strong thighs and slim hips. A black polo shirt stretches snugly across his wide, defined chest. His hair is slightly damp from the shower and the ends curl over his collar.

God, he is beautiful. So beautiful I could cry.

His eyes search the room until they find mine. Our gazes lock. My breath is stolen from me. He looked for me. *Me.*

He tears his gaze away. "Sorry I'm late," he says as he walks to his place. "I was on an important call."

"That's not a problem, good chap," my husband says with a light-hearted tone. If either Emily or I were ever late to the table, he'd rant and rave.

Dimitri takes his seat. It's not lost on me that he nudges the chair closer to Emily as he pulls it in underneath him. I get a sinking feeling in the pit of my stomach.

Dimitri proceeds to ignore me completely as he inquiries about Emily's day: was that her practicing piano earlier, what a lovely sound, how long has she been playing, would she play something for him later?

He's...flirting with her.

Bastard. He's doing this on purpose. Why would he do this?

After every single one of our scams, each time Dimitri had to flirt with an unsuspecting mark, he would bundle me in his arms and whisper over and over against my ear how much he cared nothing for them, that I was the one he loved, the one he wanted. It hurt to see him pretending, but I never doubted that his coy smile and sweet words were anything other than pretence.

Now...now I'm not sure what I think.

I sense eyes on me. Mrs Bates is standing behind my husband, waiting on orders like the lapdog she is. Usually it's a maid standing there but she's here, probably because of Mr Wolf. She's staring at me, eyes narrowed.

Shit.

I can't keep looking at Dimitri. She's already suspicious. I force my eyes down and command myself not to look at him again, despite how, like magnets to metal, they keep wanting to find their way back to his face.

Every laugh from Emily is a cut to my stomach. Every pretty thing he says to her is a stab to my heart. I want to throw up in my lap. I try to ignore it. But I can't shut out my ears.

My appetite's gone. I push food around on my plate, slowly dying inside and not being able to show it. I'm sickened by this behaviour from him. He's doing it to hurt me. It's torture, but I can't make myself leave, excuse myself with a headache or something. The deepest part of me, the part that has longed for his presence for five long years, just wants to be near him in any way possible. Even if it kills me.

Chapter Twenty-Two

Dimitri

Look at her, just sitting there, ignoring me.

I practically have Emily in my lap and yet Alena just sits there, picking at her food. She barely feels a damn thing, the heartless she-devil.

Her husband reaches over and slides a hand on hers. She looks up and smiles at him.

A stab goes through me.

What if they are in love? What if five years was enough to wash away any hold I had on her?

"Darling," he says, "would you care to join me upstairs after dinner?"

Her eyes slide to mine, a glitter of defiance in them, before she gifts her husband with a radiant smile. A smile that she used to reserve only for me. "Of course."

I almost choke at an image of crusty old Edgar lowering his body onto hers. It sears me. I grip my fork in my hand strong enough that I'm near to bending it. It takes everything in me not to throw this table aside and roar like a beast.

I seethe quietly inside. He's old enough to be her fucking father. How could she let him touch her?

"Mr Wolf?"

Right, Emily was asking something. She seems a sweet enough girl, if a bit naïve.

I turn to her, forcing a smile. "Yes, Emily."

"I was thinking of going for a walk through the gardens tomorrow after breakfast," she says in a shy tone. "Would you like to join me? We have one of the most beautiful grounds in Yorkshire. I know all the best spots."

"I'd like that," I say.

"Perfect." Emily's eyes shine with such joy. I feel a thread of guilt worming through me. She is the only innocent one here. I'm sorry she'll be caught up in my plan.

"You should come too, Mrs Worthington," I say, turning to Alena.

Alena starts, blinking at me a few times. "Me?"

"We can't tour the gardens without the mistress of the house. Isn't that right, Emily?"

I catch the look of disappointment on Emily's face before she hides it with a forced smile. "Of course you should come, Leni."

"And she will," her husband says, patting Alena's hand as if she were a well-behaved dog.

"But, Edgar," Alena begins to protest, "tomorrow I must—"

"Nonsense. Mr Wolf is our guest and you shall do whatever it takes to make his stay a pleasant one."

Alena sinks back into her chair with a nod of acquiescence.

A sense of triumph goes through me. At the same time, I want to hit Edgar Worthington for being such a sexist, patronizing ass.

Alena catches my eye and straightens, the flare of fire and defiance going through her, an echo of the girl I stupidly used to love. I glare right back.

This is who you chose, Alena. This is who you threw away our love for. I hope you regret your choice. Even if you don't, you will soon.

Chapter Twenty-Three

Alena

Dimitri spears the last piece of chicken on his plate with his fork. "This was delicious, Emily. Thank you."

She giggles like a twit. I strain not to kick her under the table, especially since we all know that she didn't actually cook anything. We have staff for that. "Thank you, Mr Wolf," says Emily. "I aim to please."

I lift my eyes—*dammit, Alena*—in time to see him gift her with one of his dazzling smiles, a smile he used to reserve only for me. "Please, call me Dimitri."

Emily's breath releases in a sigh. "Dimitri. Such a strong name."

"It doesn't sound American," my husband says.

I cringe. Even with all his money, he's an uncultured boor with no sense of much beyond the borders of England.

"It's Russian, actually," Dimitri says.

"Oh," Emily cries, "Alena is Russian too." I almost choke on my chicken. "Whereabouts in Russia are you from?"

"St Petersburg."

Emily gasps. "So is Alena! So you two could have met before."

"No," Dimitri and I both say together.

I clear my throat. "St Petersburg is a big city. Lots of people. You could grow up there all your life and *never* really know the person living beside you." I shoot a small glare towards Dimitri.

He stares back, a lazy smile on his face like he doesn't care.

"Say something in Russian," Emily begs him, "please?"

Dimitri's smile widens as he gazes at her, Russian leaving his mouth. *"Look at you fawning over me, you beautiful, naive creature."*

My stomach stabs.

"What did you say?" Emily asks him.

"I said you are the most beautiful creature in all of England."

Emily giggles, her cheeks staining pink. "Now say something to Papa."

Dimitri turns to my husband, but not before glancing at me. *"I will take from you what you took from me."*

My limbs start to drain of blood.

"What was that?" my husband asks, not a clue as to the threat Dimitri just delivered in Russian.

Dimitri grins. "I said I hope we're able to form a productive partnership."

Emily claps her hands. "Ooo, now say something to Alena."

Dimitri turns the full force of his stare upon me. "Of course. How could I forget about Alena?"

I am incensed and terrified and I hate that I am hopelessly locked into his stare, breathless for his words.

He speaks to me in Russian, his beautiful lips moving like music, so gently that it sounds like a lover's caress. But his words are velvet-coated daggers. *"You will regret the day you left me."*

My blood drains from my face.

Emily lets out an excited squeal and claps. "Dimitri, what did you say?"

Dimitri's eyes bore into mine. "Ask Alena."

"What did he say, Alena? What did he say?"

I hide my face behind a napkin, pretending to wipe my mouth, borrowing time to compose myself. I know why Dimitri is here. He's not here *for* me. He's here to make me suffer for running off five years ago. Dear God, how many times must I pay for it? How many scars must I carry because of one mistake?

I lift my chin and stare the devil right in his piercing blue eyes. I won't be cowed away. "He said, 'God gave you two ears so you can listen twice as much as you speak.'"

Dimitri's eyes flash. I stare right back, heat rising up my neck to my cheeks.

"So, Alena," Dimitri says, "if you grew up in St Petersburg, how did you meet your husband? I'm sure it's quite the love story."

I almost choke.

My husband lets out a small curt laugh. "I was on a business trip in St Petersburg. I saw her and had to have her." He doesn't mention that he saw me in Isabelle's catalogue.

"How interesting. So it was love at first sight. How romantic." Dimitri's sarcasm bites at me, but I can see that neither my husband nor Emily have picked up on it.

"And are you...married?" Emily ventures.

"No, I'm quite single."

She giggles. "How is that even possible, a handsome, charming man like you?"

"Perhaps my tastes are...too specific."

Emily rests her chin on her hand. "What does that mean?"

"I think I have a very clear idea of my perfect woman."

"Do tell."

"Well, she needs to be...imaginative, generous to a fault. She's hopeful with a dreamer's heart. A little wild like I am, and yet, she is the only one who can tame me."

The roots of my scalp start to burn. That's how he used to describe me.

He *is* describing me.

My heart begins to flutter. Here is hope alive. Here is the start of him forgiving me. Perhaps he came for revenge but our love will break through it, I know it will.

"That is my perfect woman," Dimitri continues, "A woman I would make my wife. That is, until I grew up," he faces me, "and realised that my perfect woman was a *lie*." His hateful eyes bore straight into me, piercing my hope with icy shards.

Emily lets out a soft laugh. "Oh, Dimitri. Surely you have more faith in your future wife?" She places a hand softly on Dimitri's arm. I want to rip it away.

Dimitri turns towards her and his entire countenance softens completely. Only I used to be able to soften him like that. "Sweet Emily. I'm sure you're right. I'm sure I just haven't met her *yet*."

Chapter Twenty-Four

Dimitri

The next day, I am shrouded in a cold detachment as Emily, Alena and I set out from a back door of the Worthington mansion, through their gardens. Alena is wearing jeans that cling to her slim legs and shapely hips and a thin jumper that hugs her woman's body. I feel a stab in my gut when I see her but angrily shove it aside. It's a relatively warm day by England standards, even if it is already the end of September.

I deliberately walk alongside Emily, forcing Alena to walk behind us, making her the third wheel in our little party. I can feel Alena's eyes boring into my back. I can hear the strained huffs she lets out when I gaze down at Emily. Her obvious fury feeds me, making it easy to smile.

My plan is working. She deserves it after what she did to me. How I burned over the last five years, knowing that another man was touching her, kissing her, fucking her. The wind howling through my soul like the devil was at my door. She will burn as I did. She will suffer as I did.

"Are you okay, Mr Wolf?" Emily is gazing at me with concern on her pretty features.

I realise I'm grimacing. I shove my thoughts aside and force my features to relax. "Fine. I didn't notice any pictures of your late mother," I say to distract her.

"There are none in the house."

"Why not? She must have been very beautiful to produce such a lovely daughter."

Emily lets out a wistful sigh. I can almost hear Alena choking behind me. I want to laugh out loud at each of my mini-triumphs. *This is just the beginning, Alena. Just a taste of the pain you have tormented me with these last five years.*

"I don't know," Emily says. "Papa doesn't like to keep any photos of her, I guess."

We make our way through the manicured gardens, which I dislike instantly. They're too neat and soulless, straight rows of perfectly trimmed hedges and polite little roses and posies. Emily is like a bubbly child as she points out her favourite wrought-iron bench or a treasured rectangular section of delicate pink carnations. I am forced to fake interest in them.

Emily craves order and safety, I muse. *She'd make a placid, polite little wife for a wealthy stuffed shirt.* We reach the end of the gardens, a wall of bushes separating us from the grounds beyond.

Alena has said nothing this whole time.

"What is your favourite part of the garden, Alena?" I blurt out, spinning on my heel to face her for the first time since we started walking. For some stupid reason, I want to hear her voice. I want to know what she thinks.

Alena starts. She seems startled that I've even spoken to her at all. As startled as I am. I had planned to say nothing to her and let her suffer in silence as I flirted with her pretty stepdaughter in front of her.

Alena considers me with suspicion. "I...I don't really like the gardens."

I raise an eyebrow. "No?"

"No."

"Why not?" I shouldn't be so anxious to hear her answer.

"They're too...perfect."

My chest kicks with agreement. "Where would you take me, then?"

She lifts her chin. "I'm not sure a man like you would enjoy the things I do."

I take a step towards her. "What is that supposed to mean?"

She takes a defiant step towards me, her eyes glittering with rage. "I like the part of the estate past these bushes. It turns into wild rolling moors, rough and craggy and open to the sky."

Suddenly I've closed the distance between us. "I think that sounds wonderful."

"They say the moors are haunted." I'm inches taller than her so she has to lift her chin to meet my eye. Even so, I feel like she's looking down on me. "That only pure souls can enter without fear of going mad. Is your soul *pure*, Mr Wolf?"

"As pure as yours, I suspect."

"The brambles will rip your perfect coat." She sneers at me.

I lean in. "I think I can handle a few insignificant pricks." I can smell the sun on her and the scent of her simple clean soap. It hits my lower gut, flinging me back to a time when her smell used to comfort me.

She doesn't give up any ground. If anything, she leans in too. "Your shiny leather shoes will get dirty."

"I don't mind getting dirty." My gaze drops to her lips. They part as she sucks in breath. My stomach coils with a strange heat. I remember how they used to feel against mine—so soft, so—

I shove that thought away and look up to her eyes.

"Really?" she breathes. "You look like you've not had to get dirty in a long time." She has this soft look in her eyes despite her barbed words.

"You have no idea, Alena." If only she knew what I went through to get here.

Chapter Twenty-Five

Alena

Dimitri is so close that I can smell his cologne, but underneath I can smell *him*. Warmth and safety and love, if these things had a smell. I should step back, but I can't help but lean closer, drawn in by hope. His eyes keep drawing to my mouth. Every time they do, I remember his lips on mine. I remember his hungry, intimate kisses, the way his soft tongue invaded me, claiming me, worshiping me. I know he remembers too. Something in his eyes softens and his answers lag, as if he is too distracted with remembering what we used to be.

We can still have that, Dimi, I want to whisper. *It's not too late.*

"Perhaps," I say quietly, "I have misjudged you." He leans towards me, as if he's trying to hear me better. He's being drawn to me, closer and closer, like I'm drawn to him. The air crackles between us. "Perhaps you do deserve to walk these moors."

"Perhaps," his voice has gone soft, "the moors have been waiting for me."

"They have," I admit. "They can get…so lonely out here."

"That will not do." His eyes drop to my lips again. I suck in a breath as he leans in.

"Guys?" a soft voice calls.

I jolt away from him and spin. Shit. I've completely forgotten that Emily is here, watching us now with a confused look on her face. What did I almost do? I almost let him kiss me. I almost gave us away. What excuse do I have for us being so close?

I clear my throat and turn to Dimitri, looking for his help. His face has already changed. The softness that was there is now gone, hard lines ridging his forehead, his eyes flaring with anger. As if this is my fault.

He spins on his heel and strides to Emily's side. The lingering heat of him is like a ghost.

He weaves his arm through her elbow. "Carry on, Emily. You were going to show me the hothouse next." As if nothing had almost happened.

"You…don't want to go to the moors?"

"The moors." He snorts, his voice dripping with derision. "What a stupid idea."

My mouth drops open.

Bastard.

I had forgiven him for what he did. I was prepared to overlook his behaviour thus far. But he does not deserve my forgiveness. Stupid, prideful man.

They begin to walk away. Something snaps in me. I won't be strung along like this. I won't follow along behind them like a kicked puppy.

I dart through a break in the bushes and run across the moors to get away. With the wind in my hair and the wild heather brushing against my jeans, I feel free. I ignore their calls behind me, both Emily and Dimitri.

I keep running. I run so fast I think I could take off. There's a small ruin of a castle within the grounds just over this small hill. I often go there to be alone. It is where I am queen and no one can harm me. I aim for that.

When I reach the castle, I dart inside the crumbling ruins and slow down. Two hands grab me from behind, spinning me.

"Stop running, Alena. You'll trip on a root and break your neck." Dimitri's eyes and his voice are full of angry concern. His hands, where they're touching me, burn right through me. They mark me, branding my soul.

No, I won't fall for his tricks again. He's nothing but hell's magician and I won't give myself false hope. I shove at him. "Why do you care?"

He lets go of me like I've burned him and staggers back. His hair has gone wild about his head. In that moment he looks so much like the Dimitri I used to know, I almost start crying.

"I don't care." He straightens. "I don't care at all." He turns on his heel and walks back the way he came.

Anguish bubbles up inside me and spills over. "Go on, leave!" I cry. "You're good at that."

He freezes. His shoulders tense up to his ears. For a second I think he's going to turn around. Even from here I can see his chest is heaving, his wide lats drawing in and out.

"Dimi...?"

He lifts his chin. And keeps walking. The sight of him striding away from me hits me like a knife, cutting open that wound again. I sag against a crumbling wall and cling to the stone.

Oh God, I don't think I can survive losing him again.

Chapter Twenty-Six

Alena

I slip through my husband's personal living area. I need to speak to him. I need to figure out what he knows about Dimitri. Does he know that Dimitri and I were once in love? Does he know that Dimitri was the man I wanted to pass off as my "brother"? I don't think so. But he could be hiding his knowledge. My husband is a powerful man. Would he allow Dimitri into his house without doing a check on his background?

As I approach his bedroom I can hear voices. Two voices.

I creep closer, until I'm pressed against the wall right beside the crack in the door.

"What do you even know about this Mr Wolf?" I recognise Terrance's slight nasal voice, can hear the bitterness in his tone even though he tries to hide it. He sounds a little like a boy trying to withhold throwing a tantrum.

Regardless, Terrance is asking a very good question. A question I'm desperate to know the answer to.

Terrance holds my husband's dinner jacket so my husband can slip his arms into it.

Edgar stares at himself in the mirror. It's angled in a way that I can see him but I'm not in the reflection. "I know he's rich and he wants to invest in my company."

"I'm supposed to be your advisor. You didn't even tell me you were thinking of doing a deal with him until he bloody showed up here."

My husband chuckles. "Don't act like such a jilted lover, Terrance. You are still my advisor. You still have a place by my side even if we merge with Mr Wolf."

Terrance throws his hands up. "I'm trying to look out for you. You're making it very difficult—"

"I know what I'm doing." My husband knots his tie as he stands in front of the mirror, Terrance fuming at his side.

"Do you really need *his* investment? Letting this… this *foreigner* stick his nose into the business?"

My husband flinches, just for a second. His fingers halt at his neck. Then he clears his throat and continues working on his tie, his fingers fumbling. "It would be advantageous."

"Advantageous for whom?"

"For both." The tie is unbalanced. One side is much too long and the other too short.

"I just think you're making a grave mistake inviting a communist *foreigner*—"

"If he doesn't invest, we will sink," my husband snaps, yanking his tie from his neck and throwing it over the back of a chair. He turns to Terrance, his chest rising as he takes giant breaths. "Maybe not this year, but definitely the next."

Terrance is as shocked as I am. My husband has all this old money, money passed down from generation to generation. His lineage is part of the royal line, for heaven's sake. How the hell is his company sinking?

"But…how…?" Terrance asks.

Yes, how did this happen?

How was Edgar able to keep it from his own advisor?

My husband lets out a small huff. "Does it matter? We're in this mess. I'm trying to get us out."

I back away from the door, my stomach churning. It all makes sense now. My husband is desperate. His simpering behaviour towards Dimitri makes sense.

Does Dimitri know my husband's company is in trouble? Or is his supposed investment just a way for him to slither his way into our household?

His own business advisor didn't know his company was sinking. If Edgar can hide it from Terrance, he'll be able to hide it from Dimitri. There's no way that anyone would invest in my husband's company if they knew that it was about to go under.

I must warn Dimitri.

I shove that thought away. I cannot betray my husband. My fate, Emily's fate, is tied to his fortune. If his company sinks, so do we.

Let Dimitri spend all his money saving Edgar's company. It'll be karma. Besides, Dimitri chose to come here. If he makes the stupid mistake of getting into bed with my husband, that is his own damn fault.

Chapter Twenty-Seven

Alena

I walk into the Worthington Manor library, a beautiful large room filled with floor-to-ceiling ash-wood bookcases packed with more books than I could ever read in my life. It's one of my favourite rooms. I was going to come here and read until dinner, but I start when I spot a man I don't recognise standing by the window, gazing out.

"Hello. Who are you?" I ask.

He spins towards me, a handsome man of perhaps mid-thirties dressed in a light grey suit. Long dark hair tied back in a bun, smooth, tanned skin across a strong jaw, exotic dark eyes. He smiles and it lights up his face. "You must be the lovely Alena Worthington." He walks with a slight limp as he approaches.

"I am." I shake the hand he offers me. "But I don't know you."

"I'm Javier Garcia, Dimi's advisor."

"Dimi?" I flinch. Only I used to call him Dimi.

He laughs. "Mr Wolf, I mean. Sorry, I forget that he makes everyone act so formal around him."

This man is so at ease, it's infectious. I find myself smiling at him and offering a seat in one of the chairs that are placed around a low table. I notice a tea set is laid out, steam curling from the spout of the teapot. I don't have time to think anything of it before Javier sits right next to me instead of taking the armchair.

I clear my throat. "You know Dimitri well, then?"

This earns me another laugh. "Too well." Javier leans in towards my ear. "I know all his deepest, darkest secrets."

His deepest, darkest secrets? My mind scrambles to decipher his words. When Javier pulls back, his eyes are twinkling at me. Did Dimitri tell him about me?

He can't know about me. He wouldn't be looking at me with such openness and joy.

I clear my throat. "I think that would be a very heavy burden. I hope he's paying you enough."

He breaks out into a long peal of rich laughter. "Ah, Alena," he says softly, "you are as lovely and spirited as he says you are."

Dimitri thinks me lovely? Javier must be joking. Mistaken. I can't imagine Dimitri would have any kind words to say about me based on his behaviour towards me.

But I am desperately curious now. Through Javier, I see a way to peer into Dimitri's life without him knowing. Dimitri would never tell me where he has been and what he has done. "How did you meet Dimitri? In America?"

"Ah yes. It was a few years ago when his company was just beginning to take off. He found me and plucked me from the gutters. Literally."

"Really?"

Javier nods. "He gave me a chance when no one else would. He was generous with his time, his money, and his heart. He's a good man, Dimitri." Javier's fondness for Dimitri shines clearly on his face. "He saved my damn life. I'll never be able to repay him."

I stiffen. "I see." Is it strange that I am jealous of Javier? I'm jealous that Dimitri has bestowed the best of himself on this man and reserved the worst for me. "You and I have met two very different men," I can't help but say.

Javier places a hand on my arm, his face turning serious. "Please, go easy on him, Alena. If he is cruel, it is only because he is hurting. He is not as strong as he looks."

Chapter Twenty-Eight

Dimitri

I'm supposed to meet Javier after I finished my call. He just arrived. Quite frankly, I am glad he is here. It's nice to have one person here I can trust. The door to the library, where we planned to meet, is partly open. As I approach, my footsteps falter as I hear a soft feminine voice. The source of my pain, the voice that chases me into my nightmares.

Alena is in there. With Javier.

I stop by the door, peering round the crack. They are huddled together on the couch, talking quietly together.

Something stabs me in my gut.

Javier has always had a way with people. He is effortlessly loveable and endlessly patient. That's why we have been so successful together. He is good cop, I am bad cop.

Now he's playing *good cop* with Alena. I realise I'm grinding my teeth when my jaw aches.

She says something I can't make out. He tips his head back and laughs, long and loud.

The bastard's trying to seduce her. I have my hand on the door handle before doubt smacks me in the face.

This is Javier. I know him. He would never seduce Alena. Not with what he knows about her.

It took years for the trust to build between Javier and me. After we met, he stuck around, refusing to go, putting up with me when I raged and screamed like a storm, coaxing me out when I withdrew into the blackened shell of myself. He may think I saved his life, but really, he saved mine. I *cannot* be feeling hatred towards him. I'm already stuffed with it, choking with it, drowning in it.

I see his hand fall upon Alena's arm. I want to rip his arm out of its socket and use it to beat the living shit out of him. Before I know what I'm doing I barge into the library.

Alena leaps to her feet.

Javier merely smiles broadly at me. "There you are, Dimi. We were just talking about you."

I glare between Alena and Javier. "I did not give you permission to speak to her about me."

He just snorts at me. "Don't worry, Dimi. I wasn't giving up your secrets." He winks at me, the bastard.

"You're fired."

Alena gasps, a hand flying to her lips.

Javier just laughs at me. "Oh, don't be such a sourpuss." He turns to Alena. "Don't worry, he's not serious." I want to hit him for even looking at her.

"I am," I say through gritted teeth.

Javier shakes his head, his eyes still on her. "He's not. He fires me at least once a day."

"And for some reason you won't stay fired."

Javier ignores me and keeps right on talking to her. "Truth is, he can't live without me. I'm the only one who isn't afraid of him. I know he's really a marshmallow inside."

"I'm right fucking here."

Only then does Javier pay me any real attention. He gives me a patronizing look. "Sit down, Dimi. Here," he nods towards the tea set on the table in front of him, "have a cup of tea to calm the savage beast inside. The English swear by it."

Alena stares between us, her eyes wide. "I think…I think I might leave you two."

"No, stay," Javier says.

"Good idea," I mutter under my breath at the same time.

Javier sighs. "If you leave, Alena, the conversation will become half as charming and my view will become infinitely less appealing."

I hear a growl and realise it's coming from the depths of my throat.

Alena makes her apologies as she suddenly "remembers" an errand she is supposed to be doing. She departs, swiftly, her lashes cast down as she passes me. But I can see the bob in the smooth column of her neck. I catch a whiff of her perfume. The scent of vanilla hits me in the gut like a punch. My hands curl into fists by my side.

The door clicks shut behind me, signalling that she has left the library. My fury remains.

Javier smiles at me, despite how I glare at him. "I like her."

I stiffen. "You are not paid to like her."

"She seems so different from the wretched creature who you described carelessly ripping out your heart."

She *is* a wretched creature. Don't be fooled just because she dresses so prettily and speaks so softly. "Appearances can be deceiving." I change the subject before he can argue with me. "Have you found what I asked you to?"

"Not yet." He leans forward and pours two cups of tea from a delicate white and blue china teapot. "Sit down, Dimi. Relax for one second. Here," he waves a shortbread at me, "have a cookie, there's a good boy."

I scowl, not moving towards the chair beside him. "If you haven't found what I'm looking for then why are you here and not in London?"

He shrugs and picks up his teacup, his pinkie extended. "Needed to get a bit of country air into me." As he takes a sip, his eyes slide to the door where Alena just exited. "I also wanted to meet her."

I bite down a furious retort. "Well, now you have. Get your ass back to London and get me what I need."

"Can I at least finish my tea?"

"No."

Javier chuckles. He finishes his tea and four pieces of shortbread, making a point to slurp and smack his lips, while I stand there shooting daggers at him. The damn insubordinate man. I should fire him. Again. For good this time.

Javier stands and brushes his suit down. I still haven't moved.

"Relax, Dimitri," Javier says, patting my shoulder as he passes. "No need to be…jealous." He strides out of the drawing room, leaving me alone with my tempest of thoughts.

Jealous? I scoff internally. I'm not jealous.

The memory of Javier's hand on her arm sears through my brain, making me want to run after Javier and beat him to a pulp. I grab the closest chair, trying to hold myself back, trying to calm myself, trying to steady my breath coming out in short bursts.

You are jealous. The realisation stings.

I can't be jealous. I don't want Alena. How could I after what she did to me? I just hate that she's managed to charm Javier, that's all. That's all. I know what a snake she is underneath.

I hate her, I remind myself.

I hate her.

I *hate* her.

Chapter Twenty - Nine

Alena

Javier spoke so warmly to me, and so highly of Dimitri, that after I leave him, I feel…hope. Perhaps I am wrong about Dimitri's return? Perhaps, under his anger, the same man I love is waiting for me. Waiting to take me away from this place. He just needs time. Encouragement.

But as the days go on, Dimitri ignores me. He hasn't said one word to me since that day when he burst in on Javier and me.

Javier has returned to London. I fight disappointment at his quick departure. I can't help but feel like I had an ally in him. Like, perhaps he could have shed some light on the confusing man in front of me. Perhaps that's why Dimitri sent him away.

Dimitri might be ignoring me. But he openly flirts with Emily in front of me. At breakfast. At lunch. At dinner. I can't stand his presence. It cuts me open.

And Emily, poor Emily. I can hardly stand to be around her anymore. All she wants to do is to talk about *him*. My screams inside become more and more pressurized until I can't take it anymore.

I hear a groan behind me, feel fingers on my hip, a pulse inside me. My husband has just come.

I float back into my body as he lifts himself off me. He flops onto the bed and looks at me with a frown on his face. "What have you done with your hair?"

I touch the strands by my face. It's gone back to its wild and curly natural way. "I…I haven't been straightening it lately." I don't have the patience to straighten it every morning like I had taken to doing.

My husband studies my face, his lip curling up. "I don't like it. It makes you look like a gypsy."

I shrug. I'm beyond caring what my husband thinks.

Dimitri used to love it this way. My heart lets out a small throb. I roll off the bed and head to his en suite, grabbing my robe as I go.

In the bathroom, I stare at myself in the mirror. I'm twenty-one but I feel so much older. I feel like a prisoner in my own home. Not that this has ever really been home to me. But it's as good as it gets for me. Dimitri thinks he can come in here and fuck it all up.

You are not a victim here, I tell myself. *You still have influence in this household.*

I wrap my robe around me like armour and step out of the en suite. My husband is sitting on his bed in his robe, his legs stretched out, reading glasses on his nose, and a pile of papers in his hand.

"Edgar?"

He looks up over his glasses. "Yes?"

I step closer, chewing on my lip, wondering how I should approach it. "How long is Mr Wolf staying?"

Edgar puts down his papers. "For however long it takes him to agree to a business deal."

"So a few days?"

"Weeks, more like it. Maybe even months. Who knows how long it might take for us to negotiate a contract."

Shit. I can't deal with Dimitri for weeks or months. I clear my throat and offer my husband a smile. "I just think that perhaps he'd be more comfortable staying at your penthouse in London."

"I already suggested that to him."

"You did?"

"He said that he hates the city. He'd be more comfortable here at Worthington Manor where there's fresh air and it's quiet."

No no no. It's because *I'm* here and his life's mission is to torture me.

I try another tact. "Won't he get bored here with so little company?"

"He seems to enjoy Emily's company." There's a knowing sparkle in my husband's eyes.

I wince internally. He has noticed Dimitri's fondness for Emily too.

"Regardless," he continues, oblivious to my pain, "he shouldn't be bored on Saturday."

"Saturday?"

"Didn't I tell you?" He pushes his glasses back up his nose and lifts his papers. "I'm throwing him a party."

Chapter Thirty

Alena

Saturday comes. The house is alive with people rushing about, getting ready for the party; caterers carting in trays of food, a jazz quartet tuning up in the corner of the ballroom, florists setting up elaborate displays of lilies and white roses in the centre of every table.

I've already been faking an illness the last few days so I won't have to suffer through meals with Dimitri, laughing with Emily and ignoring me.

But now I actually feel sick.

I wrap myself in my robe and walk down the corridor to my husband's chambers. I want to beg off the party. Surely, Edgar will take pity on me.

I chew my lip as I enter my husband's bedroom with a knock. He's holding up two silk ties in front of him in the mirror, one pale blue, another pale green, both of them I hate. "Edgar?"

My husband frowns when he sees me. "Why aren't you dressed?"

"I have a headache."

I'm not lying. My temples are throbbing, my hands sweaty, my heart has been an erratic mess all day. I cannot face seeing Dimitri with Emily at the party. I cannot.

"Take some painkillers."

"I have. They're not working. I'm just going to skip the party."

My husband's face twists. He drops both ties and grabs my arm, his grip too tight. He ignores my protests as he marches me out of his bedroom and towards mine, just down the corridor. "You spoiled little girl." He shoves me into my bedroom. "You will make yourself presentable and come downstairs immediately."

"Edgar—"

"I don't want to hear any fucking excuses. Do it or I will drag you downstairs myself." He slams the door behind him.

I cannot escape Dimitri. As much as I try.

Later, I fuss with my hair one more time as I stand in front of the dresser. I tried to straighten it earlier but my hands were too shaky. The best I could do was to put some product in it that would tame the frizz. Even then, my hair tumbles around my head like a violent wind has gone through it.

I smooth my hands over my dress, a red silk Valentino gown that nips in at my waist and shimmers around my ankles, and take a steadying breath. *This is your house, Alena. Don't let him stop you from being comfortable in your own house.*

I lift my chin and exit my room, the strains of the violins growing louder as I make my way through the hallway, my heels clicking against the marble. I stop at the top of the stairs to the ballroom and grip the balustrade as I survey the room, steeling myself, my stomach doing flips.

The ballroom is the most beautiful room in Worthington Manor, the grand masterpiece. It rises two storeys, chandeliers drip like a crystal canopy from the vaulted plasterwork ceiling, the hundreds of light bulbs sparkling across the black and white Spanish marble floors which are now crammed with my husband's friends, all in their finest. My eyes scan the room. Without meaning to, I know I'm seeking him out. I spot Mrs Bates hanging around the edges of the room near the entrance to the serving kitchen, surveying the crowd, making sure that every waiter is doing his job correctly, occasionally stopping one to straighten his tie or fuss at his tray. There is Terrance, by my husband's side, looking too eager to please. He just needs a collar. I spot Emily, a pretty flower standing by one of the large windows, talking to someone who isn't—thank God—Dimitri.

I spot various prominent men, men my husband knows, but not Dimitri. England's finest are here to honour their new international friend, the wealthy, mysterious Dimitri Wolf. Only I know the truth. He's not a wolf. He's a snake.

I only hope that I don't have to speak to him. Even better if I don't have to see him, but I'm not foolish enough to believe that is possible.

Like they do whenever he's in the room, my eyes find Dimitri. They lock on him. Like I am a compass and he's my true north.

God, he is stunning. I hate the way the sight of him fists in my gut. Every time. Every single time.

He's clean-shaven tonight, showing off his wide, strong jaw and chiselled features, his dark hair flying about his head. His midnight suit has been tailored to fit snugly over his strong body, a bold, cobalt shirt and matching tie underneath that brings out his eyes. He's standing with a cluster of grown men, but it's like they've all been reduced to schoolgirls, all vying for his attention, all eager, mooning eyes. He just surveys his audience with a detached coldness, an apathy that makes him all the more unattainable and desirable. At least, it looks like apathy. I know Dimitri. He's never been truly comfortable in these kinds of social situations. I can sense the suspicion underneath his studious stare, like he's trying to uncover what all these people want to take from him.

I almost snort at myself internally. *You don't know Dimitri anymore.*

The eyes of the wives and daughters standing nearby are all trained on him too, sly looks over shoulders, coy smiles over the rims of champagne flutes. Despite his beauty he seems to me like a creature from hell, his eyes glinting with blue otherworldly fire and brimstone. Like a vampire slipping through polite society looking for his prey, nobody noticing the evil that lurks within, except me.

Like he hears my thoughts, he looks up. Our eyes lock.

My heart squeezes with longing so painful it becomes difficult to breathe. My soul tugs me towards him. I clutch the balustrade lest I lose my balance and tumble down these stairs. Or worse, that I lose my senses and run into his arms. I hate myself for wanting him, despite the cruel devil he's become. I hate my heart that still hopes, waits, for the real Dimitri to reveal himself.

Chapter Thirty - One

Dimitri

This ballroom is suffocating. Packed with self-important mules and parading peacocks. All these proud airs, these marauding vanities, self-interested snakes tucked behind placid chins. They're so used to their safe, fabricated lives padded thick with old money. They have no idea what life is truly like. They would not survive a single day alone on the streets of Russia. I doubt they'd survive a day on the streets of *this* polite country. I tilt my head and feign interest in the insipid chattering of the penguins before me, even as I glance past their shoulders, scanning the crowd discreetly.

The one person that needs to be here. And she's not fucking here.

She's been avoiding me all week, a bend to my plans. She can't suffer if she's not around to watch the show. Did she manage to get out of coming here tonight?

No, Edgar would have ensured she come. I casually mentioned that I hadn't seen her all week and suggested that perhaps his wife did not like me. Then to twist the knife, I implicitly stated to Edgar that I'd be most disrespected if she didn't attend. I saw the way Edgar's eyes widened, I heard the way he rushed to assure me that Alena would be here.

I sense eyes on me, the hairs rise on my arms the way they do when I know she's watching.

She's here. Where? I scan the crowd.

Something tugs my gaze up the red-carpeted stairs to the figure at the top.

I cannot breathe.

I thought I knew what beauty was.

I was wrong.

I stop hearing what the man next to me is saying. I can't hear anything except for my own heart beating in my ears and the soft strains of the violins as they start to sing a slow song.

She is a vision in a red silk halter-neck gown that shimmers like firelight, swirling around her legs. Her hair is wild and haloed around her beautiful head, just the way I remember it. My eyes lock onto hers. I don't see them widen—I am too far away for that—but rather I sense they do. I sense the gasp that parts her lips. I can almost hear it in my ears. For this moment—the first moment in five years—I feel no rage. It falls away like the rest of this ballroom, as if it never was. That hateful beast, my constant companion for five long eternities, has been silenced. I can see straight into her, her dreamer's heart, her hopeful soul.

She begins to walk down the grand marble staircase that curls like a horn shell from the second floor to the ballroom floor. I see flashes of her slim leg peeking out through a slit of her dress. Underneath my feet, the earth moves. I find myself walking towards her, drawn to her, the insignificant crowd parting around me. She reaches the bottom of the stairs and I am almost to her. Her eyes call to me, those eyes that always remind me of leaves as the season turns to autumn. I feel something inside me…turning.

Someone cuts in front of me, blocking my view of her. Our eye contact is broken, whatever spell I was under shatters. Edgar. Edgar is the one who steps between us. Now he's telling her to dance with him. Not asking. Telling her, as if *he* is entitled to it.

Thunder rolls across my heart again. The hatred wakes from its temporary slumber as he puts his hand on her. As he pulls her in close. Over his shoulder, she catches my eye. There is something like disappointment, like sorrow in them, before she is swept away.

The bastard's done it again.

My hands clench at my sides, my shoulders tense around my ears. I have to work to keep my breathing stable.

"Dimitri!" a sweet voice calls. "There you are." At once Emily is by my side, her presence feeling like a thorn, the sharp guilt as she gazes up at me with such longing. I can sense the deep, aching loneliness in her. I can see how it gnaws at her, stripping her down to her desperate bones. I hate it. Perhaps because it feels too…familiar. I slap the guilt aside. Emily and I are using each other. Even if she doesn't realise it herself.

"I've been looking everywhere for you," Emily says, almost shyly.

I track Alena by her wild hair as she's dragged around the dance floor by that graceless oaf. At every turn, her eyes latch onto mine, a prey watching her predator.

"Dance with me," I command. Before Emily can say yes, or even blink, I've swept her into my arms and we're moving across the dance floor. Emily melts in my arms. I hear her sigh. And I tense because her shape is wrong. Her voice is too high. She smells of roses, soft, pretty. Made for manicured gardens. Not for vengeful thieves birthed from bitter streets and cut from broken dreams.

I grasp the very second that Alena sees that I'm dancing with Emily. Her eyes widen over her husband's shoulder, her head following us as she turns. I have her attention now. Good. Let the show begin.

I pull Emily even closer. She stops her nervous prattling and lets out a gasp. We are almost flush, separated by the thickness of her gown. I lean into her hair, peeking through the chestnut strands to make sure that Alena is watching.

"I don't like to talk while I'm dancing," I whisper against Emily's earlobe, my eyes burning on Alena's.

Alena's eyes narrow. She leans in to say something to her husband. Edgar laughs easily and smiles at her.

My gut stabs with anger. Those are supposed to be *my* words she carelessly spilled into his ear.

I run my lips along Emily's neck from her earlobe to her shoulder. I realise then that her gown comes off both shoulders. Emily lets out a low moan and shivers. It should be Alena shivering against me.

Alena's lip pulls up. She begins to stroke the back of her husband's neck, her fingers curling through his hair, like they used to play on me. I can almost feel them on me.

Something in me snaps. I can't fucking stand it any longer.

"Excuse me, Emily." I tear my hands off her and am pushing my way through the crowd before she can protest.

I reach Edgar and Alena, swaying uncomfortably off-beat to the music. I want to slap whoever taught him to dance. He's butchering the beat. I tap his shoulder and they break apart. If only it were that easy in real life.

I smile broadly at him and keep my voice light. "May I cut in?"

"Sure," Edgar says, at the same time as Alena cries, "No!"

She flushes red and looks away.

Her husband laughs but it's an uncomfortable sound. "She's only joking." He's watching me closely to make sure I've not taken offense.

I broaden my smile. "I imagine it's difficult for your wife to be parted from you for even a second."

Edgar's shoulders relax and he steps aside. I shove myself in front of Alena and everything in the periphery fades away. She's not looking at me, but I hear her breath hitch as I close the gap between us. She stiffens as my arm slides around her waist. My body is coursing with electricity, my vision sharp on her.

"Relax." We're not going to dance very well if she doesn't loosen up.

She snorts. "You try relaxing when you've got a boa constrictor wrapped around you."

I respond by yanking her right against me a little too roughly, my arm tightening around her. I haven't been this close to her in five fucking years, her breasts pressing against my chest, her hips against mine, sending a strange unravelling feeling through my belly. I have the gravest sense that this closeness might not be her undoing, but mine.

"What are you doing?" she hisses.

"Dancing." I direct us around the floor, swaying to the music. She fights me but I'm too strong and she's tucked in way too close to me to do anything other than to move with me.

"Of course you can dance," she mutters.

She won't look at me, but my gaze is hungry—searching each crease in her bottom lip, that single freckle on her smooth neck, each gold leaf in her green eyes.

In the background the large, golden, ornate grandfather clock chimes midnight.

"If you dance well enough at midnight," I say, without thinking.

"…the fairies will grant you a wish," she finishes for me.

Our eyes lock.

I wish…

Memories of how we used to dance in our tiny apartment in St Petersburg fill me with heat, damned confusing heat. I remember the way she used to fit against me, just like she does now. I remember my lips on hers, my hands scraping across the underside of her breasts. I smell the fresh lavender scent of her hair and I have to fight not to press my nose into the silky locks. Most of all, I remember the way my heart felt like it swelled to fit her inside it whenever she was near. She feels like the first call of light far ahead in a dark tunnel.

She feels like…salvation.

Something in me cracks, like the frozen surface of a lake under the probing fingers of the sun. The flame I once had inside me, the one that I thought had long since died, flickers alight.

I can do nothing but lean into her. We've stopped turning but my head keeps spinning. My fingers dig into her back. Her arms lock tighter around my neck. I lower my nose against her jaw and inhale. Her scent of sweet almonds and fresh soap hits my gut.

"Alena," I breathe.

She shivers against me. I feel the corners of her lips against my cheek, her breath heating my skin.

All I have to do is turn my head.

All I have to do…

The song ends and another starts up. I falter on my next step as the strains of "Stormy Weather" begins.

Of all the songs they could have played.

Our song.

Memories of that fated day in Russia slam back into me, rattling my rage awake again. No way this is a coincidence. She requested this song on purpose. She made me drop my guard just to throw it back in my face. She made me think she still cared about me.

The familiar creature takes over my body, but it cannot wash away what has risen to the surface.

I *want* her.

She made me want her. Even when all I want to do is hate her.

I pull back so I can see her deceitful eyes. "Nice song choice," I hiss down at her.

I notice too late the open longing on her face as she looks back at me. It fades as her eyes widen. "You think I requested this?"

"Don't try and tell me you didn't."

"Not everyone is as cruel as you, Dimitri." She shoves me and I let her go. She straightens. "Excuse me. I have other guests to attend to."

She turns and runs through the crowd. I stand and watch her as she disappears out the side door onto the terrace.

Something tugs in me.

You're being an asshole, Dimi. Go apologise.

Me? An old indignant voice in me screams. *I won't apologise until she apologises first. Even then, she doesn't deserve to be forgiven for what she did to me.*

I straighten my suit jacket and glance around to see if anyone has noticed Alena's sudden departure. I catch Emily's eye, standing on the side of the room, watching me. Only then do I notice Emily's wearing a royal blue dress, a colour which does nothing but make her skin look sallow. I vaguely recall that I named that colour as my favourite when she asked me the other day.

It's not. My favourite colour is that dappled green that leaves get right before autumn.

If I was smart, I'd go to Emily. She's watching me. She expects me to go to her.

Something overwhelming pulls my attention out towards the terrace. It's a force stronger than logic. An instinct. A tug on my soul. It shuts out any thoughts of plans. Of revenge.

Chapter Thirty - Two

Alena

I stand on the wide terrace, the music muted out here. Beyond me, the manicured trees and bushes of our manicured back gardens stand like solemn silhouettes, the only witnesses to my torment. I grip at the cold stone balcony, sucking in deep calming breaths, the scent of jasmine filling my lungs. Above me the moon is full. They say that the full moon makes people crazy. Perhaps, if that's true, I can blame the moon for almost losing my mind back there.

Oh my God. I wanted to kiss him. I was practically begging him to kiss me as I brushed my lips against his smooth cheek. In front of everyone. In front of my husband.

In front of…Emily. My stomach weaves with guilt. Dear God, I hope she didn't notice us.

I just… I couldn't *think* when he had his arms around me, when he was so close. Everything I buried in the depths of my soul came tumbling out around him, clogging the air.

I still love Dimitri.

I can't deny it.

Even after he's been so cruel, I still want him now more than ever. The call to throw all caution to the wind and just let him do his worst is like a fever, a disease taking over my mind and my body, making me act like his foolish puppet.

He still wants me. I know he does. I *felt* it. He still feels something even if it is buried like coals under ash, otherwise there'd be no fuel for his hatred.

Then that song. Our song. Thank God that song came on, stopping us both.

He accused me of requesting it. The hateful bastard. He doesn't trust me. Will he ever stop blaming me? Will he stop trying to make me suffer?

I hear footsteps coming up behind me and I spin. The sight of Dimitri striding towards me makes the breath jam against my voice box. By the light of the moon and the glow from inside, his eyes are wild and unleashed.

"Damn you," he hisses.

"Stay away from me," I say, taking a step back. I have nowhere to go, the balcony digging into my lower back.

He grabs my shoulders and pulls me against him.

"What are you—?"

"Five years." His eyes glitter with madness. "Five years you've haunted me. You've tormented me." His voice is so filled with anguish, dripping with such pained rage, that all my anger freezes in my veins. "You she-devil. You witch." He beats his hand against his heart. "Why are you still in *here*?"

"Dimi, I—"

He crushes his mouth to mine. My brain short-circuits. I freeze, halfway between disbelief and shock. For a moment his lips are dancing alone as they move against me, punishing me, daring me. Something rumbles awake inside me. Something that will no longer be denied. The longing and love I've been repressing for five long years breaks like a dam under the sheer momentum and fury of this blazing phoenix. My mind goes blank, awash with pure need. I kiss him back. Hungry. Desperate. His arms coil around me. I curl my fingers into his shirt and press closer. It's not close enough. I could never get close enough.

He licks the seam of my lips, begging to be let in again. I part my lips and take in his breath. Our tongues fight against each other, warring in our hot mouths. Our hearts beat against each other, break against each other. A sob tears from my throat and I feel warm rivers sliding down my cheeks. God, I've missed him. I miss him so much that it *hurts*. Even the relief cramps in my core, mixing with longing and anguish and anger. I want to beat his chest and scream at him and never let him go. Why did it take him so long to find me? Why?

He pulls away from my lips. My body begs for them back. He kisses my cheeks, licking up the salty tears. My fingers clutch at him, at his arms, his shoulders, his chest, desperate to know him again, every next part of the firm muscles I explore making the heat in my core flare.

Your husband could come out at any minute.

I don't care.

Emily could come out.

At this I pause, guilt crumpling into a ball in my chest. Her disappointment when she finds out is the only thing I will regret. But she will get over it. This not about her. This is me taking back my soulmate.

Dimitri's thumb runs across my cheekbone. His eyes, boring into mine, are pained and conflicted. "Stay with me, Alena," he whispers. "Stay with me tonight." He crushes his lips to mine again.

Tonight.

Not forever.

Just tonight.

This man is only here to hurt you, Alena. If you stay the night with him, don't think for a second he won't tell your husband. The reminder of his hateful purpose here throbs like a punch to my chest. I tear my lips off his. My hand goes flying, palm striking his cheek with a violent crack before I know what I've done.

He releases me and I stumble back, my hands now reaching for my throat. He still wants me. But he doesn't love me. He would ravage me tonight, then flaunt it in front of the only two people who care about me. This is his plan to ruin me.

I almost fell for it.

He lifts his eyes, fury glittering in those icy depths. Past the flames I see…pain, oh, so much pain. A raw, open wound. A sadness that wells so deep I cannot glimpse the bottom.

I've rejected him. Again.

My heart tears apart for him. I forget that he means to destroy me. All I want to do is help soothe his wounds. Wounds that I made. I take a step towards him, my hands reaching for him.

"Dimitri?" It's a familiar sweet voice calling from just inside the terrace door.

Emily.

Shit.

I can't let her see me here. Not like this. Not with Dimitri. Not with our kiss still splashed across our faces and our pasts bleeding from our chests. She'll *know*. It'll break her sweet little heart. She'll tell her father. And I will be ruined.

I turn and run into the darkness of the terrace. I tumble into the house through a far door. I keep running, the opulent hallways blurring around me as I speed through them, relying on instinct rather than clear sight, until I'm stumbling into my room upstairs and falling into bed, my heels kicking off to the floor.

I curl into a ball, my energy zapped too much for me to even take off my dress. It is a long while before I succumb to the darkness.

No one comes for me.

Not Emily.

Not my husband.

Not even the one I fear—and want—the most.

Chapter Thirty - Three

Alena

I feel a soft, warm body snuggling up to my back. *Dimitri?*

I let out a sigh and turn around to face him. I realise with a start that the body is too small, too soft to be Dimitri. I snap my eyes open with a gasp.

Emily is curled up beside me, her warm grey eyes fixed on mine. Despite the slight bags under her eyes, she looks awake and alert.

I sag with relief. "Oh, Emily. It's you." I rub the sleep from my eyes and glance over to the curtains stained with early morning light. It can't be any later than seven a.m.

Emily laughs and cuddles up closer to me, twisting her small feet into mine. "Who did you think I was?"

"No one," I say a little too quickly as a memory invades my mind. *His arms wrap around me, pulling me back against him. I relax into his arms. When he holds me, the warmth comes from the inside.* I shake this memory from me.

Thankfully, Emily doesn't notice. She's too busy smiling at the ceiling. "I feel like it's been forever since I've seen you, Leni. I've missed you."

A stab of guilt hits me. In trying to avoid Dimitri I've neglected her. I resolve to be a better friend, to stop being so wrapped up in my own troubles. "I'm sorry, Em. Let's do something today, just you and me, like we used to."

Her face falls. "Oh." Guilt creeps over her features. "Dimitri and I were going to take the horses out today. You can come with us, if you want?"

I can't. I can't stand to watch Dimitri dance around Emily for my sake. *Oh, sweet, innocent Emily, can't you see he's using you?* I force a smile that I know is weak. "Do you really think you should take him out riding?" Dimitri has never been on a horse. But I can't say outright that I know this. "Does he know how to ride?"

"Oh, yes. He has horses back in America."

He does? Her words stun me. I used to know everything about him. Now he is a stranger. A stranger who kissed me last night like he *knew* me.

"He's so handsome," Emily says, her small teeth nibbling on her bottom lip, "and he's such a great dancer. We danced all night last night after you left."

I swallow down a ball in my throat. "Oh?"

"Oh, Alena," she breathes, "I think I'm in love."

Emily's words stab my chest. *You can't love him*, I want to scream at her. *He's mine!* I shove this thought aside. "You... You hardly know him."

"I know enough."

Panic jitters inside me. Love? No. She can't love him. She *can't*. "But he's...he's too old for you. You're barely eighteen."

She frowns. "You were only sixteen when you married my father."

"I'm just saying, don't go rushing into things before you know..."

She pulls away, her feet untwisting from mine. Her voice becomes pebbled. "You don't think he likes me back."

I know he doesn't, I want to cry. He kissed *me* last night. He asked *me* to go to bed with him. I can't tell her that. It'll kill her. It'll ruin me. "I just don't want to see you get hurt," I say, "that's all."

"Well, I know he likes me," she cries. "He danced with me all night. And he kissed me."

My mouth drops open in horror. "He didn't."

"He did." She folds her arms, a smug look on her face.

My stomach twists with pain. Were his lips still warm from mine when he pressed them to Emily's?

Oh my God. I suck in a breath. "Did you..." oh, God, I don't want to know the answer. "Did you *sleep* with him?"

Emily scowls. "Of course not. I'm not a whore." Her choice of word tears an old wound open.

"Don't fucking touch me, you whore."

"Don't you dare call me that. I'm not—"

"Marrying a man for money? Fucking a stranger for money? Don't kid yourself at what you will become if you do this."

Despite my pain there is relief. Dimitri didn't sleep with her. He didn't take Emily's virginity to wound me. At least he didn't go that far. I sag at this reprieve. Only for a second.

Emily's watching me. "Don't you want me to be happy?"

Your happiness is a lie. "Of course I do…"

"Then why can't you be happy about me and Dimitri?"

How can I, when I know that her crush on Dimitri is *wrong*? *Oh, sweet girl, if you only knew.* What do I say when the truth will only destroy us both? "I just don't want to see you get hurt."

Emily's lips press together. "I have to get ready." She shoves the blankets off her and strides to my door, her knee-length flannel nightgown flaring behind her.

"Emily," I sit up, "come back."

She slams the door behind her.

Chapter Thirty - Four

Alena

By the time I get down to breakfast, there is only my place setting left. I sit, my eyes unfocused on the cream and rose wallpaper that dresses the breakfast room.

Coffee is set down in front of me with such a clatter that it spills onto the saucer.

I look up with a start. Mrs Bates is hovering at my shoulder.

She never serves us breakfast. Even if she did, she never serves me. She always sends one of the younger maids to do that.

She's glaring at me, something menacing in her crow-black eyes, and my stomach flips. She leans in, her eyes narrowing. "I saw you last night. You and Mr Wolf."

The blood drains from my face. She saw him kiss me. She followed us out to the balcony.

Despite the way my insides are screaming, I inject the most apathy I can into my voice. "I don't know what you're talking about."

"You looked pretty cosy dancing with him."

I almost sag into my chair. Thank God. She didn't see the kiss. "It's a dance. You have to get pretty close to your dance partner to dance." I pick up my coffee and shoot her a snide look. "Not that you'd know, seeing as nobody would want to dance with an old crone like you."

She scowls at me. "You think you're so clever. I see the way you look at him when you don't think anyone's watching. I see the way he looks at you. You never notice me watching, do you? Well, I see. There's something going on. And when I get proof I'm going to take it straight to your husband."

I stiffen. "Even if you do get proof of whatever you think is going on, what do you hope will happen when you run to Edgar? That he'll leave me and marry *you*?" I let out a curt laugh. "You're dreaming."

"You are a spiteful, hateful child. You don't deserve Edgar."

"He is Mr Worthington to you. Don't forget, you're just the help. I'm his wife."

"Not for long."

I snort. Even though I am panicking inside. I shove the saucer and cup at her. "The coffee is cold. Go get me another one." Steam is still rising from the black liquid.

"Mark my words, Alena," she hisses, "I will find out what's going on." She snatches the coffee cup and shoots me a final glare before striding away, chin held high.

I sink into my chair along with my hope. What am I going to do?

Chapter Thirty - Five

Alena

Dimitri *kissed* Emily.
He did it to hurt me.
Just to hurt me.

And oh, how he has hurt me. I am a throbbing wreck of pain. I need to stanch the blood flow. I need to cauterise these wounds. I tuck my grief away into the wooden box deep in my mind; I've gotten good at this. Later I can deal with this grief, this final loss of hope. Not today.

Today I need to force Dimitri out.

When I sneak into Dimitri's bedroom after dinner, making sure I'm not seen, he's standing by the side cabinet pouring himself a drink.

His eyes darken when he sees me, rejection flashing in them like lightning. "What do you want?"

I close the door behind me and walk towards him, my steps shaky. My hands are clammy and I have to keep wiping them on my skirt. But I have to stay strong. "I'm here to ask you, no…to beg you—"

"Alena *Ivanova* is begging me?" Dimitri leans against the wall, a cruel glint in his eyes. He lifts his drink to the air as if to salute me. "Do go on."

"Please," my voice warbles, "leave."

"Leave this room?" he asks with mock surprise.

Bastard. He knows very well what I'm asking. "Leave this house. Do business with my husband if you must, but please, leave me," *and Emily*, "alone."

He stares at me, the right side of his lip lifting in a horrible half-smile. "Get on your knees."

"*What?*"

"If you're going to beg, do it properly."

Dimitri drops to his knees in front of me. His face has cracked wide open, but it's not anger showing raw and naked on his face.

It's desperation.

"Alena," he grabs my hand, "I beg of you, don't do this."

"Dimi, I—"

"Don't marry him. Marry me."

My breath catches in my lungs. Dimitri watches me from across the room over his scotch glass. From the darkness in his eyes, I can tell he's remembering the same thing.

I stiffen. "You can't be serious."

"You want me to leave? Get. On. Your. Knees."

He wants to crush me. To wound my pride like I did his. He is crueller than ever.

You did this to him.

I'll do it if it will get him away from me, then I can just go back to my life. It was empty but at least I had Emily to love. Now, with him here, I can barely love her.

I slide to my knees. His eyes flash with fiery triumph. "Please, Dimitri. Please, leave."

Dimitri places his drink on the side table and pushes off the wall, striding towards me. My breath turns to stone in my throat as he stands right before me. I am well aware of the suggestive position I am in. His cock is at eye level, but I force myself not to look at it. Instead I look up, locked into the intensity of his stare. I know he wants to demean me. To embarrass me. My body burns with the indignity of it, and yet, heat pools between my legs.

I gasp when he places his fingertips on my cheek, a riot of sparks cascading from his touch. He brushes my hair off my face almost tenderly. My heart skitters with hope.

His perfect lips pull into a smile. "No."

The bastard. I leap to my feet, my hands in fists by my side. "You told me you'd leave if I begged."

"No," he says in a bored tone, "I told you to beg on your knees. I made no promises as to the outcome of your begging." He turns away as if to dismiss me.

My body shakes with rage. I grab his arm and whip him around to face me. "I'll tell my husband who you are. He'll kick you—"

"You tell him who I am and I'll tell him we slept together."

I gasp. "You wouldn't." My contract. If I'm deemed to have been promiscuous I lose everything. More than lose everything, I'll owe my husband a hundred thousand pounds. It's a debt I can never hope to crawl out of.

Dimitri's eyes glitter with mad pleasure. He has me over a barrel. And he knows it. "Do you wish to test me?"

He would do it too. I can see it in his eyes. "Edgar won't believe you," I try.

Dimitri grabs my upper arms with his hands, gripping me tight as vices. "Really? What are you doing in my room, Mrs Worthington?"

I struggle against him. "Let go."

He pulls me closer, crushing me against his hard body. "Go on," he says, "scream. Alert your husband to your presence in *my* room."

Bastard.

I hate him. I struggle to knee him, to kick him, but my damn skirt is in my way and he's too close to get any leverage.

He's much too close. All those old aches and wants flood back into my body. Five years I've dreamed of being this close to him again. His familiar touch, his familiar smell, his presence around me swilling like a poison. His touch burns me. He seeps into me. He sinks his teeth into my soul.

I am lightheaded. I need oxygen. I part my lips as I suck in air. His eyes dip to my mouth. Something flares in his eyes. Despite everything, he wants to give in to me too. I involuntarily lick my lips. His stare turns…ravenous.

He lets out a small hum, his lips vibrating along my skin as he traces them across my cheekbone towards my ear. "Mrs Worthington." His voice is like liquid. "Alena," he whispers, almost tenderly, sending me back to five years ago. I can feel his grip loosening on my arms but he doesn't pull away. The ache coils tighter in my stomach. His hands move up my arms, his thumbs tracing the outer swell of my breasts sending shivers through me. This soft Dimitri is dangerous, more dangerous than the cold stranger. He appears too much like the old Dimitri, the one I love. I feel my self-control unwinding, my fingers curling into his shirt, as he presses his arousal against my hip. I bite down on a moan. Despite everything, my body screams to give in to him.

"Well," his breath tickles my ear, "if I'm going to accuse you of being a whore, you might as well be one."

I shove him back. He lets go of me, laughing.

"You bastard." My breath heaves out of my lungs, my neck and cheeks flaming red. He's playing with me. Toying with me. I want to strangle him.

He smirks at me and shrugs. "At least I can admit what I am."

His words reach into my chest and twist my heart. "If you won't go, at least leave Emily alone."

"She is the one who won't leave me alone."

"*You* kissed her."

He smiles at me, cold and hateful. "Are you jealous?"

"Why are you like this? How could you be so cruel? Why do you want to torment me?"

"Why? *Why?*" His face cracks apart. "You *broke me*," he roars. "You destroyed me when you chose him over me. You filled me so full of bitter hatred, it is *all* that I taste. It's all I breathe." His voice trembles with anguish.

My heart breaks right there. His eyes so open and raw, I can see right into his charred soul. The pieces of his heart that I broke all those years ago are still jagged and sharp. With every breath he takes, they cut him, making him bleed from the inside.

"I'm sorry, Dimi. I'm so sorry."

"It's too fucking late for sorry. It's five years too late."

It can't be too late. It can't.

Love can triumph over hate. It can.

I reach out for him. My voice is pained as I beg—as I *beg*— "Dimi, please…"

"Get out," he spits, causing me to snatch my hand back. "It would be very cruel for your husband to find you here alone with me in my bedroom. We wouldn't want him to get any *wrong* ideas."

"I am not a cheater, Dimitri. Don't you dare insinuate that I am."

"Just a whore, then."

His words slap me across my face. Pain spreads from where they strike me. "Fuck you."

"No, you never did get to give that to me, did you? You gave *that* pleasure to your worthless husband."

When Dimitri arrived at Worthington Manor, my hope took flight. To see him again, after all these years, to know that he found me, that he came here for me. Even after I realised that he wanted revenge, I still believed. Even after every cruel word, I still hoped. I thought that I could get through to him. That he couldn't stay angry at me forever. I thought deep down that we would finally get our happily ever after.

But I have flown too close to the sun, allowed my hopes to soar too high. Hope has melted and my heart has plunged towards the ground, swirling and twisting, until finally crashing on the sharp, jagged rocks.

He still wants me, but he hates me more.

He will never forgive me.

He will never love me again.

Chapter Thirty - Six

Dimitri

Alena was wrong. I didn't correct her. Emily kissed *me*.

For a second I kissed Emily back. I thought it would give me satisfaction. I thought it might even be a pleasant way to pass the time here, Emily being a pretty girl. Except all I could think about was *her*.

Alena.

Alena.

Alena.

My blood beat out her name through my veins. I tore my mouth off Emily and made some excuse about not wanting to disrespect her father in his own house and went to bed soon after, locking my door behind me to make sure that Emily didn't get any ideas.

In the dark of my bedroom it was Alena's kiss that replayed over and over.

"Five years. Five years you've haunted me. You've tormented me." *The wound she made across my heart reopens, my pain spilling out and filling each one of my words.* *"You she-devil. You witch."* *I beat my chest.* *"Why are you still in here?"*

She looks at me with such sorrow. Such longing painted across her face. *"Dimi."* *Her old nickname for me stabs my heart. She makes me believe that she still might love me.* *"I—"*

I crush my lips to hers before I know what I'm doing. She freezes but I don't care. I'm stealing a kiss from her. I'm taking what should belong to me.

But when she melts against me and her lips mould to mine, my heart stutters. She's kissing me back.

She is kissing me back.

I grip her to me, my fingers digging like claws into her body, ready to tear her apart. God, she is so soft. So warm. Then her mouth opens for me, our kiss deepens and I sink a little further. My body fills with heat. Hungry, angry fire.

I can no longer deny it. I still want her. I still want Alena.

"Dimi?"

I blink, my thoughts scattering like birds. They don't go far. They circle overhead waiting to peck at me again.

Javier raises an eyebrow. "You okay?" We're sitting across from each other in the small living area in my guest room here in Worthington Manor.

"Fine." I turn back to the documents that Javier only just put in my hands. I have to focus.

I flip through the pages. My written English is not the best; that's what I have Javier for. But I know how to read numbers. "These financials are different from the ones

Edgar has given me."

Javier raises an eyebrow. "How about that."

I scan the real financials, the ones that Javier finally got his hands on. Outgoings, income, debts, assets, capital… Holy shit.

I look up to Javier.

Javier nods. He knows what I've just realised.

A smile spreads across my face, triumph tickling my belly. "Mr Worthington has been a very bad boy." Any remorse I had about crushing his company to the ground is gone.

"And…Alena?"

A sob tears from Alena and pours into my mouth. Something threatens to break out of the place I banished it to. It threatens to fill my heart.

I pull away and kiss up her tears. "Stay with me, Alena," I whisper, drunk on her. "Stay with me… tonight." I take her perfect mouth again.

She's a song in my head, on repeat.

I want her like a sickness. Even after she rejected me. I can barely concentrate on anything else since that damned kiss. The hate that I had used like a knife to sharpen my focus over the last five years was…it wasn't wavering, it was being misplaced by the thought of consuming her. Of taking her body.

Like I should have done five years ago.

Like I am owed.

I just need to fuck her. Then I can get her out of my system. She made it quite clear last night she would have no part in that. The second rejection simmers underneath my skin, mixing with lust.

I ignore Javier's question about Alena as an idea begins to percolate.

I say out loud, "I wonder how far Edgar Worthington will go to save his company."

Chapter Thirty - Seven

Alena

I refuse to acknowledge Dimitri. It's not hard during the day as he and my husband lock themselves away in his office, hammering out their deal. At mealtimes, he doesn't speak to me either, but on the occasion that I happen to look up, I catch him scowling at me like he's trying to figure something out. I don't give him anything in return—no anger, no sadness, no longing. Nothing. I am numb.

What hurts is that Emily's still angry with me. She speaks to me in stilted tones. I don't know what to do. I can't apologise for disapproving of her crush on Dimitri. I will never approve that, not just because my heart feels like it's being ripped apart when I imagine them together, but because I know that Dimitri's only intentions are hateful and vengeful.

I can't tell her any of this. I can't tell her why.

Between meals I hide myself in my study, losing myself in writing. Pages and pages come pouring out of me, like someone has finally cut me open. The feelings I cannot express bleeding onto the pages in curls of black ink.

Nobody finds me here.

Not even Dimitri.

I knock on my husband's office door and stick my head in. "You wanted to see me?"

My husband is standing at his window facing out, his hands folded behind his back. "Come in. Sit."

I frown as I take a seat in one of the plush chairs in front of his expensive wooden desk. I don't think my husband has ever asked me to see him here. Only ever in his bedroom.

"It seems Mr Wolf and I have reached an agreement."

If their negotiations are over, Dimitri will leave Worthington Manor. Twin fissures of both relief and disappointment go through me. I chastise myself for half of those feelings.

"Congratulations," I say.

Only then does he turn on his heel to look at me. His lips are pressed into a thin line, a deep frown on his face.

Something is wrong.

"He has insisted on something…unusual as part of the deal. Something that I need your help with."

Dear God. What terrible plan has Dimitri concocted now?

"Before I tell you," his voice hardens, "let me remind you of all that I have spent on your upkeep. Let me remind you of the horrible place that I plucked you from. I will not be happy if you ruin this deal for me. And in the long term, neither will you."

Edgar needs this deal. I heard him admit as much to Terrance. I study my husband's face. It's as cold as I've ever seen it. He and I don't love each other. Despite his coldness, he has been something of a companion for me. He has made life comfortable for me, despite my occasional punishments. I have never wanted for anything material, at least, while I've been here. And he loves Emily, even if he has trouble showing it, which will always endear him to me.

I nod my head. "I'm grateful for all that you've done for me."

"Good. I'd prefer you to do this willingly."

He'd prefer? He was prepared to force me if I didn't? My blood begins to drain from my limbs. "Do what?"

In my husband's grey eyes is a flash of broken pride. "Dimitri wants to spend a night with you and I said yes."

Chapter Thirty - Eight

Dimitri

I sit in the backseat of one of Edgar's cars, his driver in the front, Javier beside me. We are driving to London today to meet with Edgar and his lawyers. He is already there preparing our contract. Satisfaction coils underneath my skin. Almost there. Almost.

I remember the day when I strode into his office and made one final proposal to seal the deal. One night with Alena. I couldn't believe it when Edgar said yes. He barely blinked, just a single bob of his Adam's apple before he *gave away* his wife.

I wanted to pump my fist in triumph. Right after I bashed his face in.

Heat coils in my belly. When I return to Worthington Manor, I will have her. She will be mine.

Mine.

For only one night, an insistent voice reminds me.

Outside the tinted window the Yorkshire countryside rolls by. I've never been here before this trip, but there's something so…familiar about these lands. Rolling hills of low brush and fading pinky-purple heather, craggy crops of rock jutting out like old ruins. When the sky is grey and thick like today, the wildness of the moors feels lonely and desolate. The wind that whistles through all the cracks and caverns feels like it blows straight through my heart.

This single lane gravel road that we take away from Worthington Manor passes a low set of buildings surrounded by a low stone wall. There, I spot a familiar form. One that I would forever recognise.

"Stop the car," I demand, without thinking it through.

The driver hits the breaks, the dirt coming up around us like a cloud.

"Dimi, what is it?" Javier asks.

Alena is there talking with a man in his forties outside one of those buildings. They're standing close—much too close. Now she's handing him a basket. He takes it from her and embraces her with his free arm. My blood boils. My hands turn to fists. Is Alena fucking him too?

"Oh, it's Miss Alena," the driver says, breaking through my thoughts. I don't know his name.

"Nobody asked you," I mutter. Javier smacks my arm but I don't flinch. I don't tear my eyes away from Alena as she and the man laugh at something. Anger boils inside me. She is not allowed to laugh.

"That's the school headmaster. Alena takes the manor leftovers to the schoolkids for their lunch," the driver says in a pleasant tone as if he didn't hear my muttering. "Mr Worthington used to just have them thrown away. Such a waste. Until Miss Alena changed that." His voice is filled with affection for her.

My previous assessment of her infidelity slinks away, replaced with guilt.

"Really?" Javier says. "That's very generous of her. Very selfless." I can hear what Javier is not saying, a silent question of the devil-woman image I've constructed of Alena.

She was always so generous. Almost to a fault. The infinite heart with the dreamer's soul.

I scowl. And say nothing as I wave the driver on.

As the car passes, my gaze lingers on Alena, now kneeling beside a small boy. The image hits me in my gut, fingering my insides with longing for…

I try not to look too deeply at these unwanted feelings as I shove them away.

Chapter Thirty - Nine

Alena

Dimitri, Javier and my husband were in London all yesterday and today with their lawyers finalising the contract. I was the secret side deal, the cherry on the top, an extra perk.

Now they're back.

Tonight I am to go to Dimitri in his guest room. I am to present my body to him. Like it's some sort of prize.

I fume as I sit at my dressing table, snatching a brush through my hair. Bastard. I refused him the other night when he asked me to go to bed with him. This is his way of screwing me anyway. *Yet again, you win, Dimitri.*

I want to completely hate this, hate *him*. But for some stupid reason, my panties are damp. My core is vibrating with anticipation. A part of me *wants* to be used by him. I've dreamed of this night, fantasized about it for seven years since the day I met him.

I know that I won't go through with my earlier idea of dressing in the ugliest pair of sweatpants and most oversized shirt I can find.

I can't deny it. I want Dimitri to want me.

I hate that I want him to want me. I hate that even after all these years, after the way he's treated me, even after this insulting request, I still want him. I want him like a sickness. Like a disease.

I slip on my sexiest lingerie, a matching lace set with G-string and balcony bra from La Perla and cover it with a silk robe. My hand trembles as I drag the mascara wand through my lashes. My breath shakes as I apply my blood-red lip stain and blot.

As a single act of defiance, I straighten my hair. It hangs like a golden curtain over my shoulders. Then I slide my feet into a pair of nude Christian Louboutin heels, the red lacquer underside like blood. I square my shoulders and leave the safety of my bedroom. I sense that the woman leaving is not the same one that will return.

I don't even know how I make it down the hallway. I feel dizzy. Tipsy. I don't fear that I will be seen. The servants have been given the night off. My husband has taken Emily out for dinner. Dimitri and I are alone in this entire manor, in this entire estate.

No one to hear me scream.

I shudder at the thought, the ache growing between my legs.

When I reach his bedroom door, my heart is beating like a drum. I get one night out of my contract. One night.

Emotion wells up inside me. I have been waiting for seven years to be with Dimitri this way.

Two years of his holding back. Five years of a passionless marriage.

Dear God, I am ready. I am more than ready. I am standing at the edge of this abyss and I can't wait to fall.

Underneath, my skin trembles. I fear this night will ruin me. *One night won't be enough.*

I lift my hand to knock.

Chapter Forty

Dimitri

One night.
Tonight.
I know what I need to do and yet, I find myself pacing around my guest room. She's supposed to be here soon. And I'm as nervous as a teenager before prom.

I shower quickly and dress in freshly pressed slacks and a crisp white shirt. And I shave. I don't want my stubble scraping against her soft skin. When I find myself dabbing cologne on my neck, I scowl.

I shouldn't be giving a shit about my appearance or how I smell. She is here for me. To please me. My final triumph. My victory over her and her spineless husband. What the hell was I doing treating this like some first fucking date?

I tear off my button-up shirt and pressed dress slacks and wrap a bathrobe around me instead. What's the point in clothes? All these things I'm just going to take off again anyway.

I catch a look at my face in the mirror. I look…terrified.

I hear a knock on my door.

She's here.

I tighten the bathrobe around me.

I am in control.

"Come in." I grimace at myself when I hear the shake in my voice.

The door opens slowly. She steps inside and leans against the door after she shuts it, her fingers gripping the painted wood behind her. She's wearing a silky robe wrapped around those curves I am dying to see, a bow on the front like she's a present. My dick twitches. She is a present. She's a present to make up for the years of torment she put me through.

I take a step towards her. "You know, I was only half joking when I asked your husband for a night with you as part of the deal. I couldn't believe the worthless piece of shit said yes." My lip curls up as disgust spreads bitter on my tongue. "If you were my wife, I would *never* let another man touch you. But your husband is fine to spit on your marriage. If only you'd chosen me." I take another step towards her.

"I did choose you." She takes a step towards me, her voice firm.

"You threw me away for *money*." My hands turn to fists by my side.

Relax, Dimi. You won.

If I won, then why am I still so fucking angry?

Her eyes fill with pain, the sight stabbing me like splinters. "Dimi, I came back for you."

"Strip," I growl.

She doesn't stop her attack, her voice camouflaged as soft pleading. "All those years ago. I realised that you were the only thing I needed and I came back. But *you* were gone."

Liar. She's just trying to mess with my mind.

"I said, strip."

She stiffens, then lifts her chin. "Fine. Let's get this over with." With trembling fingers she tugs the end of her robe. It falls apart, revealing her body wrapped in matching red lace lingerie.

Curse her. She is perfect.

She is more stunning than my wildest imaginings. Soft womanly curves. Flat stomach. Long lean legs. And that defiant look in her eyes, the fire burning hot inside her. My brain short-circuits. My dick swells to painful.

My plans, my mask, it all fades away. All I can see is her.

Chapter Forty - One

Alena

I feel so exposed. So vulnerable. My half-naked body out on display for this hateful creature.

His gaze grows hungry as he drinks me in. He hasn't even touched me, he's just fucking me with his eyes. That's all it takes for my nipples to harden to painful points. A hot ache ignites in my core. My panties grow damper. And I curse him.

Even as I despise him, my body still wants him. My heart still clings to the man he once was. My soul aches to be reunited with his.

He stalks right up to me, reminding me that he is the hunter and I am prey. I keep my chin up.

I walked in here *hating* that his blackmail has me serving myself to him on a platter. Within seconds he has my body crying out for him, wanting to lie across his lap and feed him whatever he desires. He has won, in more ways than one.

"God, Alena," he whispers, "you are stunning."

My skin is so sensitised that the touch of his breath on my cheeks makes me shudder.

His fingers trace my hairline softly, almost reverently. Then down my neck, my body shivering at his touch, before he pushes the robe off my shoulders. It flutters to the ground.

He chokes on a breath. His eyes roam over me, burning me with their intensity. Who is this man? Where is the Dimitri who wants to hurt me?

He lifts his eyes and they catch mine. "You want this."

"No," I say automatically.

He laughs softly, almost mockingly. "You may have been forced to come to me tonight, but nobody forced to you wear this lovely lingerie set underneath your robe. You did that *for me*."

Bastard. My cheeks flame. "I don't want—"

"Stop playing games, Alena."

I suck in a breath as he reaches around me and unclips the bra, letting it fall to the floor. The cool air and his gaze hit my aching nipples.

He shoots me a smirk as if to say, *your nipples are as hard as diamonds.*

Okay, he's proved his fucking point.

But he's not finished yet. He slips his fingers in the sides of my panties, teasing me, his touch sending flares of heat through me. He drops to his knees as he tugs my underwear down to my ankles, making me jolt in shock.

I am naked.

Standing here in front of Dimitri on his knees.

His hands grab onto my hips, making sure I can't move. He laughs softly. "If you don't want me, little lamb, then why are you so wet?"

My cheeks burn, my body burns, as he stares right at the evidence of my lust, slick between my legs. He leans in—holy shit, he has his nose in my bare pussy—and inhales, letting out a soft groan which shivers through my core. "You smell good enough to eat."

When his tongue flicks against my clit, I jolt. A cry rips from me. He laughs again and it sounds like triumph. Before I can say a thing, he assaults me again with his mouth. Pleasure smashes through my body. My eyes roll into the back of my head and I let out a moan. He keeps licking. In five strokes he's given me more pleasure than my husband has in five years. More, I want more.

He lets go of one hip only to push my legs farther apart, giving his tongue and lips more access. I obey. I can do nothing but obey.

He wraps his lips around my clit and sucks as he flicks the end with his tongue. I moan and buck against him, pleasure tightening like bands inside my core. He chuckles before he pulls his mouth off me. I let out a whimper. For a second, I think this is his cruel plan. He's going to push me to the edge and never let me come. Oh God, I won't survive it.

Then he runs his fingertips along my seam and slips a finger into me. I let out a cry, half pleasure, half relief. A curse falls from his mouth. He adds a second finger. And a third, stretching me to my limit. I suck in a breath, trying to stay relaxed.

He starts to move, his fingers thrusting in and out, curling to rub against that sensitive spot inside me when they push deep within. The pleasure returns in waves, this time like the bass of a song, thick and low and full. A low groan rumbles from me.

When he adds his tongue again, I swear I almost die. The strands of my pleasure twisting like harmonies. I curse, I cry, I scream. My legs shake so hard, I have to grip onto his hair to stop from collapsing.

Dear God. At last. After seven years of loving him, of wanting him, and not being able to release it, at last. I let go. I give in. I come hard around his fingers, against his tongue, my head knocking back and his name tearing from the depths of my soul. I am lost in the waves of pleasure on and on until they sink like a lowering tide, exhaustion chasing after it.

I start to drop.

But I don't fall. Because Dimi is there holding me up, crushing me against his hard body with his strong arms. Even after I've had the orgasm of my life, my need is not sated. It has just been awakened. Years it has been waiting, needing, starving for Dimitri.

"You brought me here." His voice rumbles into my hair. "Even from across the ocean, I could still feel your claws in me, dragging me here."

I fix my hungry eyes on him. "Dimi—"

"Does your husband want you like I do?" He grinds his hardness against my hips. "Does he *need* you?"

"Please, let's not talk about him." We have one night. One night together. I don't want to waste a second.

"Even if he wanted you with every breath of his soul, he couldn't want you in a whole lifetime as much as I want you right now."

I moan as he rubs himself against me. "Please, I'm begging you…"

"What?" he growls. "*What?*"

"I need you inside me."

His erection twitches against me. He lets out a groan. Then pulls away. "Get on the bed."

I obey. Because all I can do is obey.

Our eyes lock, even as I circle him, backing up onto the bed. I lie back, waiting, his eyes pinning me to the sheets. He kneels at the end of the mattress and pushes my knees apart. I let them drop, exposing myself to him. His hungry eyes brush over my exposed sex. I have never been so bare, so naked. I've never been so turned on in my life. I might die if he doesn't get here and sink into me right fucking now.

He tugs his robe off and drops it off the end of the bed. Dear God, he is so perfect. So aggressively male. Rounded shoulders, sculpted lean muscles. His blue eyes flashing with wild hunger. He is so beautiful I want to cry. But it's not just his body. It's *him* I want. All of him. His mind. His heart. His soul. I want to be inside him.

Even if he and I only get tonight, it will be worth it.

Chapter Forty - Two

Dimitri

Alena lies on the bed naked, her body open for me. My body surges with so much need that I swell to bursting. As I crawl over her and slip my knees between her soft thighs, the ice wall that has protected me for so long cracks.

This is not part of the plan.

As I gaze down at her, her hair wild about her head, her eyes open and vulnerable, her lips parted, begging me to finally, finally sink into her, to surrender to her, the wall begins to crumble. Five years I've waited for her to look at me like this. Five years I hunted her ghost.

She is a conquest. A prize. That's all.

That's a lie. When I saw her yesterday, handing over food to the school, kneeling to speak with that child, this cold heart of mine began to thaw. As soon as she walked into the room, I began to lose my control.

Instead of feeling triumph, I feel raw and exposed. Naked. Vulnerable... Just like I did when I sank to my knees in front of her five years ago and begged her to choose me.

She can see it. Is that smugness in her eyes?

She planned for this. She is a siren trying to lure me onto the rocks. I can't give in to her. I know better than to hand over my heart. She will rip it to pieces. Again.

I slam my fear and lust—*everything*—into a box in the icy depths of my heart, the part that has not forgotten what she did to me. I yank myself off her so violently I almost tumble back onto the floor.

She sits up, snapping her knees shut and clutching at her naked chest. "Dimi? What's wrong?"

I stand there, staring at the mistake I almost let myself make, my breath heaving out of my lungs. I can't do this. I can't let her force herself back into my heart. I can't let her wind her claws around my soul. I will not survive a second time.

The way she's looking at me now, so full of concern, so longingly, it makes me pause. My certainty wavers.

I need her to leave before I give in. I force my face into a cold mask. "Get out."

"W-what?"

"I changed my mind. I don't want you anymore."

"Liar! You want this. You want *me*." Her anguish is like a knife twisting in my gut.

I rip my eyes away from her, afraid that I won't be able to resist throwing myself at her if I keep looking at her.

Dimitri Volkov does not beg.

I keep my voice cold, even as my heart screams in my chest. "I thought I wanted you. Turns out, having you just bores me."

I see the moment her heart breaks. I see it shatter behind her autumn-leaf eyes.

I should feel good that she's hurting. Instead I feel like a piece of shit.

She grabs her robe, snatching it around her body. She picks her lingerie up and stuffs it into a pocket. "You are such a bastard." She strides past me, the scent of her perfume mixed with the musk of her lust hitting my lungs.

"No," I yell after her, my voice coming out all needy and defensive. "You are Frankenstein. And I am your monster."

My door slams in response.

Chapter Forty - Three

Alena

I can barely look at Dimitri at breakfast the next morning. My husband can barely look at either of us. I didn't tell him that I didn't stay the night in Dimitri's room. I didn't tell him that Dimitri ripped my heart out instead.

I want to hate Edgar. I do a little. But he's desperate. I can smell it on him. I know he had no choice but to hand me over.

All my hate centres on Dimitri.

Dimitri scowls at me. I can feel his glare, boring into me like it could set me alight. He's furious. But I have no idea why. *He* was the one who rejected me last night. I was there, naked and open and ready for him and *he* rejected *me*.

My stomach still burns with it. I try to console myself that I never really wanted him anyway. I try to tell myself that his rejection means nothing. *He* means nothing to me. Not anymore.

Then I look up and find Dimitri's eyes are filled with sorrow. They glisten with what looks like regret. Confusion tumbles around in me and I have to tear my eyes away from him. So what if he regrets last night? Who cares if he's sad? I just want to hate him. It's easier to just hate him. Anything else is too damn painful.

Only Emily chatters away, oblivious to the silent tension strung among the three of us.

After breakfast I leave the manor to visit the local school with my basket of leftovers. I walk. It's not far. And the weather's still mild, although overcast.

As I turn onto the slim laneway towards the school a familiar figure slips out from the gates ahead and into a waiting car.

I halt, the gravel crunching under my feet.

That was Dimitri. I'd recognise his stern walk and proud figure anywhere. What is he doing here? The car pulls away and drives off in the other direction, leaving a cloud of dust in his wake.

He hadn't seen me.

Anger slithers through me. Why was he here? What business of his was it to come here? This is *my* place, the one good thing in my life that he hasn't tainted.

Yet.

The blood drains from my limbs and I almost drop my basket. Surely—*surely*—he wouldn't be so cruel as to destroy a school just to punish me? He couldn't hurt all these children. Oh God. What has he done? *What has he done?*

I run, ignoring the basket slapping against my hip. I keep running until I reach the headmaster's office, bursting through his door without any announcement.

Richard starts in his chair, looking up from behind his desk. "Oh, Alena."

I heave in breath, my lungs struggling to suck in enough air, cramped by my effort and fury. "Dimitri Wolf was here."

He blinks. "Why, yes—"

"Why?" I stride up to his desk and drop my basket to the floor. Richard is a kindly man in his mid-forties. He's been headmaster of this school for almost a decade, having attended this very school as a child. He would never let Dimitri destroy this place, would he?

Dimitri is good at sniffing out people's weaknesses and using them. Just like he did with my husband and his failing company. Just like he's doing with Emily and her silly crush on him.

Richard and I are friends, or at least, I thought we were. Now as he squirms in his chair, avoiding my eyes, I have to question it.

Dimitri is messing with my husband's company, he's driven a wedge between Emily and me, and now here… My blood boils. He can't mean to take *everything* away from me, can he?

After what you did to him five years ago? I shove this guilt-thorned thought aside.

"Why did Dimitri come here?" I lean over the desk, my palms flat on the surface. "Tell me."

A frown appears between Richard's brows as he meets my gaze. "I'm sorry, Alena, but the purpose for Mr Wolf's visit is confidential."

"If it has something to do with me, I have a right to know what he's done," I squeeze out through gritted teeth. "If you were ever a friend to me, you have to tell me."

"You?" Richard's frown deepens. "Alena, you're mistaken. His visit had nothing to do with you."

I straighten up behind his desk. "Then why was he here?"

Richard sighs and gets up from behind his desk. He walks over to the door that I left wide open and shuts it, turning to me. "What I'm about to say hasn't been announced yet, so you'll keep it to yourself."

"I... Of course."

"Dimitri Wolf has donated enough money for us to refurbish our library."

"What?"

He nods, his face bursting with the joy of being able to share such wonderful news. "He came here to ask what needed to be done to the school. I told him about our recent need to raise funds for the library."

I had tried to help with that. I had begged my husband to let me donate the money they needed, but he refused me. I have no money of my own to give. I'd secretly gotten the help of the cook and the kitchen staff in baking an array of cakes for a bake sale. It had been a success but it had only raised less than five hundred pounds. Not nearly enough.

Richard grips my arm. "Alena," his voice lowers to a hush, "Mr Wolf just handed over a check for ten thousand pounds!"

"*What?*"

"It's more than enough for the library upgrade. We'll have money left over to upgrade our science lab and our gymnasium. Oh, Alena, he is a Godsend. Is he a friend of yours?"

I sink into one of the chairs in front of Richard's desk. I can scarcely believe what he's saying. Ten thousand pounds!

Why did he do that?

He did it for you, Alena.

I shove that thought away. "Did...did Dimitri say why he donated all that money?"

Richard shrugged. "Only that he was inspired to do it after he drove past the other day and saw our grounds."

I have misjudged him. Completely. I have to thank him. I have to apologise...oh God, the names I called him. The accusations I hurled at him. How nearsighted I have been. He *is* still the same Dimitri underneath. He's just hurting on the outside. He let himself get close to me and he got scared.

"Alena, you can't tell him you know he was the one to donate the money."

I look up to Richard. "Why not?"

"He made me promise not to reveal it was him. I only told you because you just looked so terrified at his intentions. I know you can keep a secret."

I nod, my head spinning.

I'm in a daze as I make my way home after dropping off the food I brought. How am I supposed to act now when I see him?

My heart is softened towards him. But I can't reveal that I know.

This proves he still cares for me. Dimitri still cares. Underneath his cold, ruthless armour, he is still the warm, caring soul I love. He's just a wounded animal lashing out in pain. I just have to find a way to open his heart. I have to find a way to bring the old Dimitri out. I won't give up on him.

I arrive home forty minutes later and one of the maids opens the front door of Worthington Manor for me. I rush past, throwing my light coat and scarf in her arms. "Is Mr Wolf in?"

"Yes, miss. He's in the formal living room, but—"

"Thank you," I call over my shoulder.

I burst into the living room, a stately room centred around a low antique table and enough seating for over a dozen. I come to a halt. Dimitri is here, yes. But so are

Emily and my husband.

"Ah, Alena," Edgar says, "you're here. We have some wonderful news."

I glance at Dimitri. He looks stern and a little pale as he sits next to Emily, but it doesn't take away from his beauty. I yearn to run to him and throw my arms around him and thank him for what he did for those children. But I can't. For so many reasons.

"Really?" I say. "What news?"

Emily curls her arm through Dimitri's. "We're engaged."

Chapter Forty - Four

Alena

I let out a laugh. "Be serious."

Emily looks a little miffed but she forces a smile and presses closer to Dimitri's side. "I am."

It's then that I notice how close they're sitting. Their bodies pressed side by side. Cold realisation travels through me like a deadly frost.

This is a joke.

A nightmare.

A mistake.

My gaze snaps to Dimitri's face. "Dimitri? Is this true?" He won't look at me. I see his insides churning even from here. I remember the way he looked down at me last night, how the fear stole across his face and he leapt back as if I had burned him. Oh God. What has he done?

"Of course it's true," Emily says.

My head spins. I can't say a thing. I am too much in shock. I grip onto the sides of my dress because I need something to hang on to.

Dimitri looks at me. "I know Emily looks upon you as a sister. That'll make me your new *brother*, won't it?"

My brother. His words are a direct attack. They pierce me through my chest.

He has not forgiven me. He is not done making me suffer.

"Won't you congratulate us, Alena?" he says, his words soaked in bitter triumph.

I force a smile even though my heart is breaking. "Congratulations." What a sham this engagement is. They won't go through with it. They can't. "When is the happy day?"

"In four weeks," says Emily, beaming up to Dimitri.

Four weeks.

Oh God. He means to go through with it. Just to hurt me? Or…has he really fallen for Emily?

I swallow down the ball of thorns in my throat. I stagger over to the closest chair and sit. "Sorry," I say, my hand pressed to my stomach, "I'm just overwhelmed with the news. This is all so sudden."

"Actually," Dimitri's voice is cold, "it's been inevitable for some time."

This was his plan all along. He manipulated his way into our lives, he seduced Emily in front of me. This was all to hurt me. This was all for revenge.

Anger thunders through me. Well, let him ruin his own life if he wants. Let him marry a woman he doesn't love. At least he won't be around here anymore.

I choose my words carefully. "Four weeks. I see. Then you'll move to London, I suspect."

Dimitri smiles and pats his fiancée's hand. "I'm sure Emily won't be in a hurry to leave her childhood home. We'll stay here until we find a suitable house nearby."

"Nearby?" I choke out.

"Of course." His eyes glitter with triumph. "We wouldn't want to move away. We're all going to be one big, happy family, after all."

Dear God. My nightmare is not over. It's barely begun.

Chapter Forty - Five

Alena

I corner Dimitri alone in the corridor in front of his guest room. I grab his arm and swing him to face me. "You can't do this. You can't marry her."

His features are cold as he stares down at me. I almost don't recognise his man. "I'm afraid I can do exactly as I like."

"What about last night? Before you freaked and threw me out? You felt it, I know you did. You still love me."

His eyes narrow. "You seem to be under some misguided belief about my feelings for you. Let me make it clear." He grabs my arms and pulls me in close, so close I can see the flecks of pale ice in his deep blue eyes. Despite the rage bubbling in me, I can't help but remember how his bare skin felt against mine last night. Desire fissures through me at his nearness. "I may have had a moment of weakness, but believe me, that impulse is over."

"No," I shake my head. "You're trying to dampen what you feel by marrying her. You're trying to pretend you don't care. But you do."

His lip curls up. "You shattered my heart five years ago, Alena, you ripped my soul into pieces. Your suffering is all I care for."

"Then hurt me if you want to hurt me. Leave Emily out of it. She's done nothing to you."

His eyes drop to my lips. "I will hurt you. I will hurt you every time I kiss her. Every time I hold her close or whisper in her ear." He pulls me flush against his hard body. His breath tickles my ear, making me shiver. "It's your turn to go to bed every single night, your soul tearing to pieces as you imagine me fucking someone who isn't you."

His words hit me like bullets from a firing squad. Pain, unlike anything I thought I could feel, rips through me. I shove him back. He lets me go. His face blurs behind tears making him unrecognisable.

I want to hate him. I do. But I can't help but imagine Dimitri all those years ago suffering like I'm suffering now as I married someone else. Now I understand his madness. Now I understand his rage.

I turn and run.

Chapter Forty - Six

Alena

"Edgar," I tumble into my husband's bedroom. He's standing at his window, staring out across the grey misty moors. "You can't let this happen."

He turns to look at me, his face twitching. "Let what happen?" he says slowly.

"You can't let Dimitri marry Emily."

Guilt flashes across his face, which he quickly covers up. "I've already given him my blessing."

I can't fucking believe this. "How? *How* could you give me to him last night then agree for him to marry Emily today?"

"I have no choice, Alena," my husband says, his hands running through his hair. "Dimitri is saving my company, saving us. I have to give him what he wants."

"Money isn't worth losing your daughter to a monster."

"You've never had to work for money," he snaps, "you just spend it. You live comfortably under my roof, eating good food, wearing designer clothes and you don't consider for a *second* what I must do to provide it for you. You have no idea what work is."

His words are a slap in the face. I stumble back, more pieces tearing in strips off me. He's right. It's true. Dimitri took care of me when I was younger. Then I let my husband take care of me now.

All the fingers I've been pointing outward begin to turn back in. This situation I've gotten into, I brought on myself. I've been reaching for the easy answer all this time. And I've left myself dependent. I'm not free. I'm caged.

Chapter Forty - Seven

Alena

My husband won't stop this wedding. I must. I can't let Dimitri ruin more lives than my own.

I tumble into Emily's room, where she's sitting behind her dressing table humming to herself and running a brush through her hair. She spins, rising to her feet like she's a floating dandelion bloom, a huge grin spreading across her face. "Alena, isn't it wonderful."

"You can't marry him," I blurt out. Shit. My desperation is making me blunt. I had all these calm, sage words to say to her but they all flew out of my head the instant I saw her dreamy face.

The smile drops from her face as the happiness bleeds out from her. Her mouth parts. "I can't believe you would say that to me."

I ignore the guilt. Hurting her a little now is much better than sitting back and letting her go through with it. "I'm only saying it to stop you from making a mistake. You've only known him for four weeks, Em."

She shakes her head as she begins to pace, her hands in fists by her side. "What does time matter when you're in love. You married my father after only knowing him for a few weeks."

I cringe. Emily doesn't know I was *bought*. "That's different."

She spins towards me, her arms crossing over her chest. "I thought you were my best friend. Why can't you be happy for me?"

"How can I be happy that you're marrying a man who's cruel and hateful and—"

"He's not cruel. He's kind and caring."

"You don't know him like I do."

Emily stiffens. "You're jealous."

"No!" I protest a little too quickly.

"Yes, you are. Just because my father doesn't love you, you're jealous that someone might actually love me the way *you* want to be loved."

"He doesn't love you," I snap. I regret it instantly.

"And you think he loves you?"

I flinch.

Realisation flashes in her eyes. "You do, don't you? You want to take him from me because *you* want him." Her lips press to a thin white line. "You jealous, spiteful bitch."

She's seen right through me. Underneath the concern for her, the need to save her from a loveless marriage, is the belief that Dimitri is *mine*. He is mine, no matter what he has done or what he has become. "He's not *yours*, you stupid girl."

The doors burst open. Edgar strides in. "What's all this noise here?"

Emily straightens, tightening her crossed arms. "Alena doesn't approve of my marrying Dimitri. She…" *wants him for herself.* I feel her eyes slide over to me, a clear threat of exposing my true feelings to the man I married. I stiffen, but I don't beg her not to speak. "She's saying all these awful, untrue things to try to stop me."

I lift my chin. "You know my feelings on the matter," I say to Edgar. "I won't stand by and watch you destroy this family." I play the only card I have left. "Either she goes or I go."

"What?" Emily and my husband say together.

Dimitri is determined to destroy the ones I love and they're letting him do it. I can't stop any of them. But I can't be around to watch it. It will kill me. "There's not enough room for two mistresses of Worthington Manor. Either Emily leaves this house or I will."

Emily lets out a small gasp beside me.

I keep my stare focused on my husband. If she leaves, Dimitri as her fiancé will have to go with her. Either way, I will not have to watch him use her.

As Edgar looks between Emily and me, his daughter and his wife, his face grows from shock into a cold detachment. "Then it is clear. You can move out, Alena. You will stay in the cottage in the Cotswolds."

I let out the breath I was holding. Emily has gone silent beside me. I suspected my husband would choose Emily. She is his daughter, after all. Still, my heart cracks. I want someone to choose me. I want someone to choose me over everything.

I nod, biting back the sting of tears. "I'll pack my things now. If your driver is free, I'll leave first thing tomorrow morning."

Chapter Forty - Eight

Dimitri

Early the next morning, just as the dawn breaks, I stand by the window of a small front study on the third floor opposite my guest room. I watch as one of the servants walks out the front carrying Alena's single suitcase.

I thought she would have packed more.

Then again, Alena never asked for much.

The servant places her meagre item into the trunk of the car that is to take her away. I've looked up the distance from here to the Cotswolds. It's a three-hour drive away but it might as well be across the Atlantic.

"Are you really going to let her go?"

I spin on my heel. Javier is standing at the doorway. "You're right. It would be more satisfying to watch her suffer if she stays, but what can I say to convince her to stay?"

Javier shakes his head. "For an intelligent man, you really are an idiot sometimes."

I grit my teeth, my hands curling to fists by my side. "That is no way to speak to your boss."

He snorts. Javier has never been intimidated by me. No matter what I do.

Neither has Alena.

He walks all the way in, letting the door swing shut behind him. "She's still in love with you."

"Good. It'll make my—"

"And *you* still love her."

"No." I bat away his words. I don't love her. I hate her. For all the suffering she put me through. I have a plan. I need to stick to the plan.

"Go after her. Stop her."

"I'm not here for her," I explode. "I'm here for revenge. I'm here to make her suffer. And my plan is working."

Javier's disapproval radiates off him. He takes a long, deep breath. "I've been by your side for a long time, Dimi. I've stood there while you've done some questionable things. But this...this has gone too far."

"Leave if you don't like it," I snap.

Javier's face cracks with pity. The bastard thinks he knows what's going on. He thinks he can see through me. "I'm not going anywhere. You should know better than that." His words slide into the cracks of my armour. My jaw stings. I want to say so many things to him. But I...I just *can't*.

I turn away. There's something lodged in my chest and it's making it hard to breathe.

"I'll be in my room if you need me." Javier's footsteps move towards the door.

I see from my window that Alena is standing by the open door of the car looking back at the house. I think she sees me at the window watching her. For a moment, our eyes lock. My heart tugs towards her. My stomach twists with a creeping kind of horror.

She can't leave.

I imagine myself running after her. I don't know why. I don't care if she leaves. I don't fucking care, you hear me, heart?

"Dimi?" Javier has paused at the door. "Don't fight so hard for revenge that you lose everything you need to be happy."

Chapter Forty - Nine

Alena

The backs of my eyes sting as the driver pulls away from the front of Worthington Manor and down the carriage driveway. I'm filled with mixed feelings. Worthington Manor has been a home for me, Emily has been family. I know that even Edgar, despite his detached, sometimes cruel manner feels affection for me.

Neither of them have come out to say goodbye, both of them choosing to do it last night after dinner.

Dimitri didn't say goodbye. He didn't even look at me once during dinner.

I tuck these thoughts away and wipe under my eyes. I turn around to watch as the manor disappears. My heart twists when I see Dimitri standing outside the front door, watching me go.

My exile is a five-bedroom stone house in the Cotswold district, three hours south from Yorkshire, cold and dusty from months of non-use. My husband has let me know that he will send a housekeeper to me soon. Percy, his driver, unloads my single bag into my bedroom, tips his cap to me outside. "You'll be missed back in Worthington Manor."

"Thank you, Percy."

"Mrs Hobbs baked you her famous shepherd's pie. I put it in the fridge for you to reheat later."

I nod, blinking back tears. Apart from Mrs Bates, my husband's staff were always kind to me. They too, had been a kind of family, I realise. One which I didn't fully appreciate until now.

Once Percy drives off, the car kicking up gravel and dust behind him, I am alone.

Alone with my thoughts.

I walk through each bedroom, opening windows, airing out the rooms. It's so quiet here. So quiet. I walk to the room that is to be my new bedroom. It has plenty of space and a nice view over the back garden. I can't see the surrounding area like I could from my old bedroom window, a stone wall sitting rudely in the way.

I unpack my suitcase slowly, my thoughts ever flying back across the moors to Dimitri and Emily. Guilt weaves through me. I left her alone with him.

I tried everything, I try to reason with the guilt. I begged Dimitri not to go through with ruining a young girl's life for the sake of revenge. I tried to get Edgar to disallow the engagement. I ruined my friendship with Emily trying to get her to turn him down.

There was nothing more I could do. Dimitri won.

If I stayed I would only be making myself suffer and giving Dimitri an audience.

I turn and start at the figure in the doorway.

Chapter Fifty

Alena

I drop the shirt I'm holding, my hand going to my throat. Terrance is standing in the doorway to my room.

"Terrance." I force my voice not to shake. "Don't you know it's rude to sneak up on people?" I was so lost in my thoughts I hadn't heard his car come down the front driveway. I hadn't heard him enter or move through the house. "What are you doing here?"

Terrance smiles, and the sight is cold and cruel. "I know who Dimitri really is."

My skin prickles. I pick up the shirt I dropped and brush it off, acting as coolly as I can, even as my heartbeat speeds up. "I don't know why I should care."

"Dimitri Volkov." Dimitri's old name from his mouth sends a crackle through my spine. Terrance stalks into the room. "Your ex-lover." The walls feel like they're closing in with his steps. It's getting really hard to breathe. "I wonder why neither of you have revealed that you know each other."

He stops right in front of me, closer than appropriate. The look on his face is mad with glee. He has me and he knows it.

"What do you want, Terrance?" I try to push past him, I need air. He grabs my arm. I wince, tugging against him. His hand squeezes like a vice. "Let go of me."

He leans in close, his acidy breath in my face. "What will you give me, pet, if I keep your little secret?"

"You want to blackmail me? I have no money."

"Ah, but it's not money I'm wanting from you." His eyes travel down my body. Oh my God. He wants… Bile rises into the back of my throat. Real fear grips my body with its claws. My closest neighbours are at least two miles down the road. Even if I scream, they can't hear me.

He yanks me against his foul body, his free hand clamping down on my breast. I let out a scream and draw back my knee and thrust as hard as I humanly can. My hard kneecap connects with his crotch. With a pained grunt, he lets go of me.

I don't hesitate. I run.

I run out of the room, into the corridor, right into a hard wall of muscle. I look up. Relief and a feeling of safety flood my body.

"Dimitri," drops from my lips like a whispered prayer.

His chest seems to swell and he wraps his arms around me. I sink into his warmth.

"You little bitch." Terrance stomps into the corridor. His halts, his face contorting when he sees Dimitri by my side.

Dimitri pulls me behind him, a low growl emanating from him.

Terrance's face quickly pulls into a sneer. "Dimitri. Fancy seeing—"

Crack. Dimitri's fist collides with his nose, his arm moving so fast it's a blur.

Holy shit.

Terrance lets out a yelp as he stumbles back. I gasp, my hands flying to my mouth.

Dimitri grabs Terrance's blood-splattered shirt and slams him against the wall. "If you ever threaten her again, I'll break more than just your nose."

Terrance gurgles as blood rushes down his chin. "You can't threaten me. I'll go to the police. I'll—"

"And tell them what? That you tried to rape a woman?"

"I'm an upstanding member of this community. No one will believe you two dirty foreigners over *me*."

I suck in a breath, my nerves jangling. Terrance has connections to people in power. If he went to the police, we'd lose. Dimitri will get thrown in jail.

Dimitri's lip curls up, his eyes glittering. "You breathe a word of this, *any* of this, then I shall tell the world about *your* dirty secrets… Prostitution. Gambling. The fact that you *stole* money from your own business partner."

Terrance's eyes boggle out of his head. "H-how…?"

"You think you're the only one who can do a little digging? Now, get out. Before I change my mind and snap your neck."

Chapter Fifty - One

Alena

The front door slams behind Terrance. A motor starts and gravel crunches as he tears away, his engine fading until the silence is a heavy throbbing in my ears.

Dimitri stands there looking at me. I stare past his shoulder at the sweet cream wallpaper dotted with tiny violets, my heart too scared to hope. "What are you doing here?"

"I broke off our engagement."

My gaze locks with his. God, his stare is too intense. It's fire to my soul. "So soon. Is Emily okay?"

"She's young. She'll get over it."

"Why—"

"She's not the one I want," he stalks towards me. Unlike earlier with Terrance, my body blooms with heat. "I want...I *need* you."

My heart drums against my ribs. I back up against the wall, Dimitri's body enclosing me in. He smells so damn good, his musky cologne invading me as his heat and his presence and this *need* conquers me.

"I wanted to hate you. I wanted to hurt you. But you..." His soft hands cupping my cheeks contrast against the sharp anger in his voice. "You bewitch me."

There it is. The admission I've wanted to hear for weeks makes my chest ache with relief and...impossibility. My eyes flutter shut as I struggle to retain my self-control. "Dimi, I'm married."

His lips brush against mine. "Leave him. Be with me."

My core coils with heat. My fingers curl into his shirt. I moan as my body wars with my mind. "But my contract..."

"I'll take care of it."

My eyes snap open. Dimitri has never looked so serious. Oh my God. He'd pay the hundred thousand pounds to my husband for me? "You'd do that...for me?"

"Of course I would. Everything I've ever done—good, bad, ugly—has been for you. You have to know that."

Something cracks inside me. The last five years of repressed anguish and loneliness releases in a flood along with the last five weeks of pain and torture.

"Alena," he hushes, kissing up my tears as they roll down my cheeks. "Don't cry."

I need him. I need his mouth on mine. I just *need*.

This time I'm the one lunging for his lips. Hungry. Needy. His tongue finds mine in my open wanting mouth and I moan. His hands twist into my hair as he presses me farther into the wall. My head spins like we're on a carousel as my hands roam his body, learning the shape and feel of him again. God, he feels so good. The hard planes of his strong muscles. The way my arms barely fit around his back. The way he presses his hard length against me.

He breaks away from me and I whimper.

"I am not fucking you for the first time against a goddamn wall," he growls.

I nod. He's right. We've waited this long. What's a little longer? My mind turns to a large bed, soft sheets, low lighting and Dimitri making love to me all night.

He slides his hands behind me and grabs my ass, breaking through my thoughts. He lifts me so that my legs are wrapped around his waist and my sensitive core is pressed against his hardness. I groan at the sweet, sweet pressure, my world turning on a long-forgotten axis as he carries me into the bedroom and lowers me to the floor.

His hands make quick work of my clothes and his. I reach for him, wanting to touch his beautiful naked body. He grabs me before I can, spinning me. He lifts me onto the edge of the bed and presses my back down so I'm on all fours. My entire being is alive, electric with anticipation. I gaze at the painting at the head of the bed, a landscape of the lonely windswept moors at the end of autumn, mottled purple like a fading bruise.

I gasp as his erection finds my entrance. His fingers tighten on my hips as he pushes inside me. He feels so full and…right.

My head spins. I've waited seven years for this. Seven long years. Is this truly happening? Is this real?

He begins to move, hard and violent, his pace relentless. I grip the sheets as pleasure and the need for more crash against each other. He is brutal and furious. He fucks me like he hates me. I push back. He fights back. Maybe he needs this, *we* need this. A violent ballet of limbs and groans. There's plenty of time to make love later.

"Never leave me again," he growls, as he slams into me like he wants to break me apart.

"Oh God," I cry, as we race towards the edge.

"Say you'll never leave me." He grabs my hair and pulls so my head is forced back, making my scalp tingle. His breathing is heavy and hot in my ear as he covers my body, his chest against my back, his thrusts unrelenting. "*Say it.*"

"I'll never leave." I can't hold it back anymore. My body shatters into a million beautiful pieces. And I scream, "Oh God, never, never, never."

I feel him pulse inside me and he lets out a long vicious groan as he comes apart too.

We collapse in a heap, a ruin of hot breath and sweaty limbs.

Chapter Fifty - Two

Alena

I trace my fingertip along the ridges of Dimitri's stomach as I lie naked along his side. Inside, I feel a sense of peace I have not felt in years. My restless soul has settled, now that its other half is back. I feel whole.

I should feel guilty. I know I should. I have a husband. But he never loved me. And I never loved him. Our marriage is a sham. What exists between Dimitri and me lies beyond the realm of mortal laws.

When I look up, Dimitri is watching me, his eyes hooded, a half-smile on his face. I flush. "You came after me," I say.

"I watched you leave and..." he swallows, "it was quite possibly the hardest thing I've ever had to do."

He came after me. He put his hate aside. My heart warms. "Harder than becoming a millionaire investor, Mr Wolf?" I tease. I haven't had a chance to dwell on this accomplishment until now. Dimitri did everything he set out to do and more. I'm so proud of him.

"Yes." His eyes are serious. There's no trace of bragging. "Making money is just about numbers."

"And you know numbers."

Dimitri says nothing. The silence swells with missing time, with the five years that we've been apart. I want to know everything about that time. What he did, where he's been. I want to stitch our lives back together again, starting from when he left Russia.

"Where did you first live in America?"

His lips twitches before he answers. "New York."

New York. Like he always planned. I imagine Dimitri as a nineteen year old arriving without me in that strange foreign land, only the simplest of English words to his name, and my heart twinges. "Did you—?"

"I don't want to talk about that, okay?" He slides out from under me and stands, flashing me a view of his perfect rounded ass, before tugging on his briefs.

I sit up, clutching the sheets to my chest, a strange feeling scraping out my chest. "Where are you going?"

He turns to face me, his glorious chiselled body on display. I think I see a flash of something dark cross his eyes. It's gone before I can even be sure. "I can't just lie here. There are things that need to be done first."

"Of course." He's right. What we just did was disrespectful to my marriage, sham as it is. I need to end my marriage before Dimitri and I can start our lives together properly. We need to tell my husband and...Emily. My stomach pangs. I toss aside the sheets and reach for my clothes. "I'll pack so we can leave—"

"No. Stay. Relax." He pulls me into his arms and kisses my head. "I'll go first. I'll explain everything to Emily and your husband. I'll send the car back for you tomorrow."

I melt into him, chewing my lip. "They'll be mad. Hurt."

He nods against my hair, swaying with me a little. "I'll take the brunt of it."

My heart lets out a flutter. "You don't have to face them alone."

"It's better this way, Alena. Trust me." He leans in, claiming my mouth in a deep kiss. A kiss that has my toes curling and wild heat dancing in my body again. He pulls away before we can get carried away again. "Soon everything will be right."

I smile up to him. "Everything will be perfect."

Chapter Fifty - Three

Alena

The car arrives the very next morning as Dimitri promised. I'm ready, my single suitcase packed. On the long drive to Worthington Manor, I have nothing to do but to think about how Edgar and Emily reacted when Dimitri broke the news to them yesterday. I am achingly happy Dimitri is mine again, and the rightness of it has me beaming so hard that my cheeks hurt. And yet, underneath are tangles of regret.

My husband's pride will be hurt, but he will move on quickly. I'm not his great love, not even a little love. I'm nothing more than a vessel for an heir for him.

But Emily...

I should have told Emily about Dimitri. I should have told her long ago. Perhaps her heart might have been spared. But I was too scared that even speaking his name would unleash the tight control I had on my hurt. I was scared that she'd tell her father and expose me. And I was embarrassed at my mistake. Ashamed at myself. I could not bear for sweet little Emily, the only friend I had, to gaze upon me with disgust or pity. I'm no fool. I know women judge each other more harshly than they do men. It's easier to forgive Dimitri for all his faults than to forgive me for a foolish mistake I made five years ago when I was just a child.

My palms are sweating when the car pulls up in front of Worthington Manor. I let out a shaky breath as I gaze across the familiar structure. I didn't think I'd be back so soon.

The front door opens. My heart leaps.

It's not Dimitri. It's Javier. His face is dark and his lips are pressed thin and white like a lightning strike.

I tumble out of the car without waiting for the driver to open my door. "Javier, what's wrong?"

He calls to the driver to take care of my suitcase and takes my arm, leading me towards the house. "Dimitri has taken over Edgar's company."

"What? Edgar would never let—"

"He has no choice. Dimitri secretly bought up the majority of the shares." Javier shakes his head. "It was an underhanded move. One that he didn't even let me in on."

The flash of darkness in Dimitri's eyes yesterday. Oh God.

This isn't over.

We walk quickly into the house. Inside the air seems hot and thick. I can hear the distant sound of wailing.

Emily. My stomach twists.

I start forward to go to her but Javier holds me back.

When I turn to him, his face is bleak. "That's not all."

My stomach drops. What more is there?

"This house, in fact all the property Edgar owned, was put up as collateral against his company as part of the reinvestment." Javier's throat bobs. "Now that Dimitri owns the company…"

"He owns this house," I finish for him.

"And he's given Edgar and Emily twenty-four hours to leave the premises."

My hands fly to my mouth. No. He can't. He…

He can. He would. The hatred I thought he had let go of was only lying underneath the surface. Waiting for this moment.

He planned this.

He planned everything.

"This is your fault," a voice hisses. I look up to find Mrs Bates halfway down the stairs, her hands gripping the balustrade like claws, her eyes, fixed on me, are filled with bitter hatred. For once I cannot blame her. "*Whore!*"

"Mrs Bates," Javier reprimands in a stern voice. "Speak to her again like that again and I shall have you removed from this premises without the courtesy of allowing you to pack your things."

Mrs Bates looks like she wants to say more. But she shuts her mouth and stomps away with the swish of her skirts.

Javier turns to me. "This is not your fault, Alena."

I nod numbly, but I don't believe him. I am the reason for the monster that lives inside of Dimitri.

"It's not too late to stop this. If anyone can get through to him, it's you." Javier grips my hands, his dark eyes fixed on mine radiating with worry. "He's in his bedroom."

Chapter Fifty - Four

Dimitri

I run my fingers over the papers on the desk in my guest room, soon-to-be master bedroom. This was not part of my plan.

But as the car took Alena away two days ago, something broke to the surface inside me. I'd run through the house like a madman before I knew why I was running, tumbling out the door, staring after the car in the distance, already too far, a piece of my soul flying alongside it.

I'd fallen in love with her again. With her wild spirit, her generous soul and her dreamer's heart. Or maybe I'd never fallen out of love. It had just been buried underneath the world of pain I had carried on my shoulders.

I was good at foreseeing things. It was the reason I had risen so fast. Loving her was not something I foresaw.

I remember sinking into her body yesterday, into her soft, wet folds. For a split second, I felt peace. I felt the pieces of my heart stitching back together.

Only it wasn't enough. It was never enough.

The anger is still here, the hungry beast. I'd fed it for five years and it grew fat and greedy.

Someone still needs to pay.

And Alena…

Well, I have different plans for her now. She still loves me. She regrets choosing him, this much I know. But her love is not enough. Her promises not enough. This time, I'll make sure she'll never be able to walk away.

Chapter Fifty - Five

Alena

Dimitri is standing behind his desk when I enter his bedroom. His head snaps up to me as soon as I walk in, even though my feet barely make a sound on the carpet, nor does the well-oiled door creak. I didn't knock either. It's like he can sense me. He can feel the pull our souls have on each other and probably always will.

I shut the door behind me. "Please, don't do it."

"It's not up for discussion."

I shake my head, refusing to accept it. I walk in farther, moving closer to him, slowly, the way I would an injured animal. "Why, Dimi?"

"Your husband dared to take you away from me."

"He didn't know I was someone else's to take."

"And what about now? I see the way he treats you, Alena. Like you're worthless. When he should be worshipping the very ground you walk on." His hands flex into fists so tight that his knuckles go white.

No. Please no. My blood chills in my veins. "You can't have done this for me. I don't want this, no matter how badly he treats me."

His eyes narrow. "I did this for *me*."

I must find a crack in his defences, a chink in his armour. I know Dimitri isn't heartless like this. Not truly. "What about Emily? She's done nothing to you except love you."

Dimitri's lip presses just a touch. "She doesn't love me. She doesn't know me."

"She doesn't deserve to be kicked out of her childhood home without a place to go."

"It's nothing personal with her. She just got caught up in the *sins* of the people around her."

My heart stabs. Dimitri has not forgiven me. Yesterday as he was taking me, even as he was giving me the most intense pleasure of my life, he was still punishing me. Would he ever stop punishing me?

"Hurting Emily is unfortunate but necessary," he says with such coldness, it pierces my heart.

"It is *not* necessary."

"It is." His fist slams down on the desk. "My heart—my fucking world—was shattered five years ago. Someone must pay." His eyes glitter with madness. "They *will* pay. I *will* have my restitution."

All my hopes turn to ash in my mouth. I've failed. He will not listen to me. He can barely hold my gaze without scowling.

He slides a pile of papers across the desk towards me.

"What's this?"

"For you."

Me? Dread fills my stomach with bile. I pick up the papers, my eyes scanning across the black ink. I didn't think my heart could drop any further. I didn't think my world could crumble any further.

I was wrong.

"You said you'd never leave me," Dimitri says. "Forgive me if I don't take your word on it."

My visions blurs. It's a contract. Dimitri has drawn up a contract for me, a marriage contract. It binds me to him forever. No divorce. No release clauses. No loopholes.

He wants to make sure I never leave him.

Chapter Fifty - Six

Alena

I float aimlessly down the corridors, the folded marriage contract burning a hole in my pocket. I needed time to read through the pages, I said to Dimitri. I think I said. I'm not sure.

I jerk out of my thoughts when I pass my husband's bedroom. Through the crack in the door I can hear a voice. And…is that a sob?

I creep closer and press my eye to the gap.

My husband is sitting on the floor with his back to me. In dress slacks. I gape at this alone. *So undignified*, I can still hear him saying when he found Emily and I lying about on the carpet in her room.

Edgar is muttering something, his voice breaking, to the large framed photo in his hand.

I swallow a gasp. He's holding a photo of me. One I've never seen before. When was that taken? Why is he holding it?

Then I notice that her hair is straight, the tip of her nose more upturned and her cheeks are a touch softer than mine.

It must be his wife. Elise. The woman whose name he calls sometimes when we are together.

She and I could have passed for sisters.

A piece of the puzzle slots into place and I can see the whole picture. This is why he wanted *me*. Because I look like Elise. My husband still loves a woman who is dead. Emily's mother. My heart twists in my chest for him. This is why he is the way he is. Edgar resents me for not being *her*. He must hate himself for trying to replace her.

My husband's cold facade shines differently in my mind. For the first time in five years, I see him for who he really is. Not a monster. Not the villain in this story. But a person who lost the love of his life. A person who made poor, grief-fuelled choices.

Not so different from Dimitri.

Or…me.

Chapter Fifty - Seven

Alena

I stand at Emily's closed bedroom door, staring at the engravings of choked ivy painted in placid cream. I've been here for God knows how long, trying to work up the courage to go in. I'm not sure how many times I lift my hand to push open her door, only to let it drop to my side.

Go to her, Alena. She needs you.

She hates you. She didn't even say goodbye properly when you left here two days ago.

Regardless of what has happened, regardless of how she feels about me, I cannot just walk away.

I take a deep breath and open her door. Emily is sitting on the edge of her bed, staring out her window. Her face turns towards me as I call her name softly.

"Alena." Her red-rimmed eyes widen as she stands.

I prepare myself for her fury. I steel myself as she storms over to me.

She throws her thin arms around me and sniffs into my shirt. "I'm so glad you're here."

I push aside my surprise and grip her back, pressing my face into her rose-scented hair, warmth trickling into my heart. "I should have come sooner."

"I shouldn't have let you leave." She pulls back so I can see her face.

I wipe her soft cheeks and push forward a smile despite how my heart hurts.

"I was so blind about Dimitri," she says, her voice quiet. "You tried to warn me. Why didn't you tell me who he was to you? I never would have agreed to marry him if I knew he was your ex."

"I'm sorry." I truly am. I can see how much I have treated her as a child until now. She can handle more than I thought. "I should have told you."

"Best friends don't keep secrets, Leni."

My chest squeezes, tears rim my eyes, and I nod, suitably chastised. "You're not mad at me?"

She sniffs, forcing a smile. "I am. But we're best friends. Sisters. We forgive each other." I tug her into another hug, relishing the warmth of her. I don't think I could bear it if I lost her. "Whatever happens," she says into my hair, "we'll be together, right?"

I squeeze my eyes shut as my heat grows heavier.

She doesn't know about the contract Dimitri offered me.

Chapter Fifty - Eight

Alena

"Have you signed the contract yet?" Dimitri strides into my bedroom the next morning without knocking.

I turn from the window, where I've been trying to capture this view in my mind, and face him. Beautiful Dimitri. Standing firm and unmoving, confidence and assuredness rolling off him. He looks as comfortable here as his own home. It is his home now. He is the master here.

I avoided him all last night, choosing to eat dinner alone in my room. I needed time to think. And now, I *know* my mind. I know my heart and I know my soul. Perhaps for the first time in my life.

I fold my hands in front of me. "I loved you more than anything, Dimitri. I made a mistake five years ago, running away from our argument. But *you* are the one who gave up on me."

"I heard you, Alena," he bursts out. "'He's nothing but a thief and a simpleton. He's never going to be anything more.'" My blood frosts over as my old shameful words fill the room. He heard me spilling my raw, unfettered hurts to Natassia. "And my favourite," Dimitri continues, "'It would *kill me* to marry Dimitri.' Well, I showed you, didn't I?"

That's why he left St Petersburg. That's why he left me.

I almost laugh. Look at what we've done to each other. Just because we were both so rash, so wild, so…thoughtless five years ago. All this because of a tragic twist of fate.

"Oh, Dimitri," I say softly. "You only heard the half of it. I realised as soon as I said them that my words were lies. I turned back for you. I came back to you but you were gone. I didn't leave *you*. You left *me*."

"Lies!" He strides up to me, his hands in fists, his face turning red. "Stop trying to make this my fault. *You* did this."

Even now he won't *see*. He can't.

He's spent so long blaming me it has become like his shadow. Like the ground underneath his feet.

My body swells with pity, pushing out any residual anger. I cannot hate him even after all that he's done. I cannot hate him like he hates me. Hate feels like a dagger aimed out, but it is really the poison coating the handle, soaking through your skin and into your blood.

"I waited for you for five years," I say, my voice calm despite the raging of my heart in my chest. "But now I know…the man I love is dead." My voice struggles around the knot in my throat. "I don't know who you are."

I lost my Dimitri long, long ago. I paid for that mistake.

But if I marry *this* Dimitri, if I sign a contract binding

me to the stranger standing before me, I will pay for that mistake forever.

I square my shoulders, my soul filling with steely resolve, and pick up a small bag from my side. I arrived at this manor with nothing but a lifetime's worth of guilt and regret. I will leave with a single bag and something much more important than material goods.

Dimitri's eyes drop to the bag in my hand. I see the moment when he realises what I'm doing. The anger shatters on his face, his hatred abandons him, revealing the scared little boy underneath. "*No.*"

"Goodbye, Dimitri." My voice cracks on his name as I begin to walk, despite my feet feeling like lead. Despite my heart breaking.

For the last time in my life, I leave him.

Chapter Fifty - Nine

Dimitri

She's bluffing.

This is a way to get me to negotiate terms in our marriage contract. Clever girl. It's what I would have done. Even as Alena passes me, I remain stoic, my mind a fuzzy whirr.

The door clicks shut behind her, leaving me alone in her bedroom. The scent of her sweet almonds and vanilla lingers like a ghost.

I don't know how long I stand there. Staring at the door. Waiting for her to come back in.

Seconds. Minutes. Hours.

"Goodbye, Dimitri." Her voice cracks, the anguish leaking from her words...

...is real.

She left.

Something snaps inside me. The part of me that she hadn't broken now shatters. Now everything that is whole is a cruel mockery. My hand reaches for the closest object. It smashes against the wall in a shower of ceramic before I realise it was a vase. The table is next. I barely feel the weight of the solid wood as I slam it into the floor, pieces snapping off, splinters digging into my palms.

She said she wouldn't leave me again. She lied.

I throw the record player across the room and smash the vinyl record, our only record, on the floor. That song, our song, was just a lie. Every word from her mouth, a lie.

Nothing is safe from my violent limbs. I break. I smash. I destroy everything I can grab, everything not tied down.

She made me want her again. Devil woman. She made me want her then she threw me aside when she was no longer interested, playing with me like a fucking toy.

The photos of us—of her, of me, of us—set in frames over the rickety mantel get knocked over with one violent sweep. I can't stand the sight of her smiling at me. The smashing of glass echoes inside my soul.

I tear the sheets off her bed, kicking the mattress at the same time. The bed scrapes across the floor, pillows flying across the room. I tear and tear, feathers scattering from me, every violent rip echoing the sound of my heart in her hands.

I rip open the box containing her birthday present. What a fool I was to think she loved me like I loved her.

I spy the edge of a box under the bed. Something she kept hidden. Something she left behind. I want to rip out her darkest secrets and watch them burn.

I snatch it out and fumble with the lock, my fingers jerking with agitation. It's fucking locked.

No key.

Where's the key?

Fuck the key.

I stride over to the marble side table and smash the lock against the corner until the lock yields.

I shake the box open and the contents tumble out onto the table.

The slip of torn white lace. The shard of vinyl. And a photo of me.

Pieces of the apartment I destroyed in St Petersburg.

Truth spears my heart with cold accuracy. I stumble back from the broken ghosts of my past. She was telling the truth. She did come back all those years ago.

Just because she came back, it doesn't mean anything. Remember what she said. *Remember she chose* him.

All strength drains out of my body and I collapse to my knees, heaving in breath. I can't seem to muster any more anger.

Chapter Sixty

Alena

When I step out the front door of Worthington Manor, Emily and Edgar are standing there clinging to each other. Edgar is so pale and shaky that I think it's Emily who is holding him up.

The car is waiting for us, Percy standing by the open trunk. "I'm sorry, Miss Alena," Percy says to me, his voice low.

"Me too, Percy."

He takes the duffle from my shoulder and places it in the trunk. "The new master has allowed me to drop you off somewhere. Where would you like to go?"

He's asking *me*? "I…"

I turn towards Emily and Edgar. They're both staring at me as if they're waiting for me to say something. They're looking to me to figure something out. *Me.*

Right. I fold my sadness away, like I'm so good at doing. I will deal with it properly when I have a moment. But not now. My family needs me now.

I clear my throat. "I know where to go."

Chapter Sixty - One

Alena

"Thank you, Richard," I tell him again. He is letting Emily, Edgar and me stay in the tiny gardener's cottage on the school grounds in exchange for doing some work about the place. Just until I find a proper job. Just until we can get on our feet again.

Richard nods and pulls me in for a quick hug. "I can't believe what Mr Wolf did. He seemed to have such a good heart."

"He does." I pause. "But he's too sick with anger and revenge that it can't shine through."

"I hope he realises soon what he's done."

I don't tell him that I think it's too late.

Richard glances over my shoulder. "Will they be okay?" he asks in a low voice.

I glance back. Edgar is sitting slumped in a sofa, a bottle of cheap wine in his hand. The only movement he makes is to drag the bottle up to his lips and gulp. He doesn't even bother to wipe off the drops of wine that dribble over his chin and onto his expensive herringbone shirt, his tailored jacket now flung across the back of the chair.

In this tiny cottage there's only one bedroom with a small double bed which Emily and I share. Edgar will have to sleep on the couch for the first time in his life.

Emily has stumbled out into the back garden like a zombie. She's left the back door open and a slight breeze chills the inside. She's never had to worry about closing doors to keep the heat in before.

I've been dirt poor before. I'll survive. But Emily and Edgar? Both of them have only known comfort and riches. Neither of them has ever had to want for anything.

I turn back to Richard. "They'll be okay," I lie, forcing a smile.

After he leaves, I walk quietly over to Edgar. He's nearly passed out now, his eyelids droopy. I tug the near-empty wine bottle from him. He grunts and mumbles something. I hope this will not become a habit of his. I hope for his sake. And for Emily's.

After I dispose of the bottle, I walk out into the garden and sit next to Emily on the wrought-iron bench positioned in a small patch of sun.

"What happens now?" she asks, her voice empty and hollow. It hurts me to hear her voice like this.

"Well, I get a job, then a proper place to live. Life doesn't end when you stop having money."

She stiffens. "I see. And what happens to me?"

I blink at her. Emily's mouth is pressed in a thin line. Her hands are fists in her skirts and she's glaring at the overgrown grass.

"What do you mean, what happens to you?"

A tear rolls down her cheek. "I knew you would leave me. I knew it."

"Emily, what are you talking about?"

"Now that Papa doesn't have all his money you have no reason to stay."

"Emily, I'm not leaving you," I say, horrified.

"I know about your contract with my father," she blurts out. "You were going to leave him when you had a baby and got his money. I'm not stupid."

My stomach stabs. Emily did know after all. She did know and she never said.

She never said.

I never told her.

"Emily," I grasp her hands, "you are my family. I would never leave you. If you want, you can come live with me once I get on my feet. You're an adult now. Your father can't stop you."

"You're lying."

"When I got the money for the baby, I was going to ask you to come with me. You, me and the baby."

Emily's face snaps to mine, her eyes wide, her mouth parted. "You…" Her eyes fill with water, which turns into fat tears that roll down her cheeks.

I brush those tears aside with my thumbs. "What did you say earlier to me? We're best friends. Sisters. We will always love each other, no matter what."

She flings herself into my arms and I hold her close.

For the first time in the last five years, I feel like I've done something right. Even though it hurts, I am taking my life into my own hands. With every breath, my strength grows.

Chapter Sixty - Two

Dimitri

A few days later…

In the manor, I walk like a ghost through the rooms, as stark and empty as my soul. Mrs Bates resigned. Not sure where she is now. I told the remaining staff to take a holiday, paid them to leave me in my despair.

The dust is settling on all the old-fashioned tables and cabinets that are not at all to my tastes. The wallpaper is too damn fussy. I could redo all these rooms. Get them all upgraded, all styled in my own way.

Then what?

Somehow, I know they'll still be as soulless as they are now.

For the first time in my life, I don't know what to do. There is nothing to aim for. I have no goal, no burning ambition. Without Alena to strive for, to fight for, to live for, what do I do now?

I stumble into a small room I've never been in before. Heavy wooden bookcases adorn the walls, filled with books, so many books. There's a desk facing the window overlooking the moors, a comfortable chair seated behind it.

It's Alena's study. I know it's Alena's because the scent of her perfume hangs in the air. I know because it's the office she always wanted.

A proper wooden desk.

Stacks of paper with lines.

And pens. Lots of pens.

It's her office.

I lower myself into the chair that she used to sit in, run my fingers across the desk. I close my eyes and let myself imagine her here, writing away.

I open my eyes. There are pages of lines written in pen scattered across the desk, more balled up in the wastebasket. I shouldn't look through her things. It feels so private. But it makes me feel closer to her. Now that I've destroyed any hope of happiness with her, it's as close to her as I can ever hope to get. I slide open each drawer, looking, seeking, like a hungry child, for a glimpse of her.

I find a stack of papers, a page on the front titled *Beautiful Revenge*.

Is this…a manuscript?

I pull it out, placing it on my lap as if it contains the secrets to the heavenly kingdom. I turn over the first page and begin to read.

It's a love story. The story of Dante and Ana.

I swallow back the rising ache as I read over scenes that are too familiar to me. This is our story. Alena's and mine.

Dante and Ana.

Dimitri and Alena.

I keep reading, half mad, half possessed, desperate to relive our lives again, even though I know how this tragedy ends.

My fingers crinkle the edge of the page as I dive into the moment that changed everything…

"I have to accept the Englishman," I say to Natassia, the GW's dark-haired receptionist. Even as I say these words, my voice sounds hollow. I squeeze my eyes shut, but every time I do, I see Dante on his knees in front of me. I remember my cold words to him and they spear me through my heart. I snap my eyes open and focus on Natassia's face, her lovely features drawn into a look of concern.

She and I are sitting on a wrought-iron bench in the courtyard of Isabelle's agency, so the girls inside can't hear us. She is the only one here who knows the truth about Dante. That he's not my brother. She's promised not to tell. I don't trust her, exactly. I don't know her. But I had to talk to *someone*. I just have to hope that she keeps her word.

"What I wouldn't give to leave this horrible place," I spit out. "What I wouldn't give to have a better life." I just want to know what it's like to be warm and fed and happy. I want to know what it means not to have to worry all the time. Is that too much to ask for? Bitter frustration bubbles up within my well of hurt. "If Dante can't see that…he can stay here and rot, see if I care."

Anguish surges through me again as I relive this painful moment. *You said you came back, Alena. But here is your proof again that you threw me aside.*

Wait…there's more.

A sharp wind blows and the creak of the front gate sounds out of the passageway. Natassia slides a hand onto my shoulder. She has been so kind to me since I first came here. "If that's how you truly feel, then go and make your slice of Heaven with the Englishman."

I remember Dante's face as he called me a whore. He will never agree to this arrangement. I know him, once he forms an opinion, he won't let it go. My chest wells up with such a sharp emotion that I stop breathing for a second. "Why does Heaven seem to cost so much?" I ask, barely a whisper.

It costs me...Dante.
I have to give him up.

The thought slashes through me, a lightning strike trying to cleave my soul in two. It illuminates our past, our history, the very intertwining weave of our two lives. There's no joy that Dante and I both don't share. No pain that we don't live through together. A realisation strikes me with such force I double over, sucking in air.

Dante and I are two parts of the one soul.

He *is* my soul.

How can a full belly be satisfying if my soul is left hungry? How can I truly be warm if my heart is left cold? What sapphires could please me more than Dante's eyes? What symphony as rich as his laughter? What finest silk could compare to being wrapped up in his arms? All the world could crumble and wither into ash, but if he were still alive, I'd still be happy.

Suddenly the rain and mist inside me clears. Everything is clear and fresh, like the first day of spring.

I look up from my hands, twisted together in my lap. Natassia is frowning at me, asking if I'm okay.

"Oh, Natassia," I breathe, "I've been such a fool." My blood rushes with purpose, my veins swollen with

clarity. "I need to find Dante." I fling myself from my seat and begin to run, my soul feeling like it has remembered its wings, now taking flight.

I stagger back from the desk, the papers slipping from my hands, scattering like scared doves. The realisation of what I've done feels like death's blow.

I have been the fool.

I had all these chances to listen to her—truly listen to her—but my ears rang with insult. I had all these chances to see the truth, but I kept myself blind with revenge, clinging onto my bloated pride. I had all these days to grab onto her, to reach for our future, but my hands were too filled with hate.

It's not furniture and stuff that fills a home, but laughter and voices and love.

All those things had been in my grasp. I let them slip through my fingers. I let *her* slip through my fingers.

I've lost her.

I've lost her forever.

I have only myself to blame.

Chapter Sixty - Three

Dimitri

I pull all the pages together and read the rest of the manuscript. It's good writing. Raw and wild and passionate. It's Alena all over. My heart squeezes with every page, my eyes sting with pride. I always knew she had it in her. Always.

"You can do anything, Alena."

I read all the way to the last page in one sitting. After I finish I sink back into the chair that she once sat on.

In Alena's story, "Ana" falls pregnant and has a boy that she names Dante Junior. She gets her money. The next time her husband is away on business, she takes her baby and "Emma" with her to the USA. She finds Dante, begs his forgiveness. And…

Ana gasps as she gazes up at me. "You…you forgive me?"

"Of course." I brush my lips across hers. "After all, that's what love is."

This was what Alena dreamed of. This was what she wanted. Me, as part of her family.

What I wouldn't give to have this fairy-tale ending. I would give my entire fortune. Everything I own.

But life is not like fairy tales.

I am not the prince who gets his princess. I am just a short-sighted fool.

There is a knock on my door. "You called for me?" Javier's familiar voice fills Alena's old office, where I now spend my days.

It still smells faintly of her. I run my thumb over the ink smudge on the wood. It's the size and shape of Alena's thumb. My thumb now rests where hers once did.

Javier stands in front of her desk. "Dimi?"

She used to call me Dimi. I look up. "How is she?"

He blinks. "Who?"

"Don't play dumb with me. I know you've been keeping tabs on…" I work my throat around the knot. "Alena." Her name sends another stab of hurt through me.

Javier nods. "You know me too well."

"So?"

"She's doing okay. She has a job now, administration work at the school. It doesn't pay much, but they're getting by."

I nod. "She's a survivor." She can survive anything.

Even...me.

Alena doesn't want me anymore. I could not give her a family. But I would be damned if I wasn't going to give her the only other fairy tale she's ever dreamed of.

"Javier, I need you to do something else for me."

"Yes, sir?"

I nod to the pile of papers on the desk. "Find a publisher for this manuscript."

Javier frowns. "You wrote a book?" He steps up to the desk. His eyes widen when he sees Alena's name on the cover page that I printed out and placed on top.

"*Don't* say a word," I warn.

He shuts his mouth.

"When you get an offer—and only when—tell Alena. Give her the offer. But don't tell her that I did this. Tell her... Tell her that you found her manuscript. That you found a publisher behind my back."

"Dimi."

"Whatever you do, *do not* tell her it was me. Understand?"

He pauses. I know what question is coming. "Why don't you just tell her that you're sorry? That you want to make it up to her?"

I wince as my heart throbs. "She doesn't love me anymore, Javier. I made sure of that. I've caused her so much pain. I don't want to cause her any more. The best thing I can do for her is to never let her see me again." I turn towards the window and look out across the lonely moors, now drained of colour. "No amount of sorrys will ever redeem me for what I did to her. She deserves to be happy. I will do everything in my power to make sure that happens. I just...I can't let her know. She's so damn stubborn." Despite my pain, I smile. "She'll never accept my help if she knows it's from me."

"But wouldn't—?"

I slam my fist on the desk. "I don't pay you to question me, dammit, just fucking do it."

Javier's only reaction to my outburst is to smirk at me. "Actually, I think you do pay me to question you."

I let out a groan. "Well, don't. Not with this. Please."

Javier studies me for a long moment. The bastard always thinks he's so clever, reading into all the things I do.

Before I shout at him to fuck off, he nods. "Consider it done." He heads to the door, manuscript in hand.

"And Javier?" I call after him.

"Yes?"

"Make the necessary preparations for us to move." I turn to watch the wind playing across the moors, my thumb still playing with Alena's fingerprint ink stain. "I can't bear to live here anymore."

Chapter Sixty - Four

Alena

A few days later…

I walk alone along the road from school to our cottage. This way is longer but I like taking this route home because it's more scenic. It has nothing to do with the fact that it passes by the low brick wall that runs along one side of Worthington Manor. Nothing. I don't care to see Dimitri again. I just…like to check on the manor. To make sure he hasn't burned it down in all his rage.

I stop today at the wall near the top of a small hill. From here I am mostly hidden, but I can see the front of the massive building, the driveway, and the road that the driveway turns onto. I frown. The windows of the manor look dark. All the curtains have been drawn. I can see the cluster of cars in the circular driveway and people swarming about. I squint and try to make out what they are doing. Two familiar figures step out of the front door. I would recognise Dimitri's figure anywhere. The other must be Javier.

I gasp and duck behind the wall. *Stupid, Alena. He can't see you from there. Why did you duck?*

I wipe my sweaty palms on my skirt and slowly stand. He's gone. Where did he go? The car in the front of the convoy sets off down the driveway. The other cars are still there. They're packing up the cars full of suitcases and boxes. I suddenly realise what's happening.

The first car is now almost to the end of the driveway. Dimitri is in there, I know it.

He's leaving. Dimitri is leaving.

No. Before I realise what I'm doing, I'm running. I'm running for my life towards the road. My heart thunders in my ears, my legs scream with effort. I'm not sure why I'm running, I just know if I don't, I will regret it.

I'm almost at the small gate that separates the school grounds and the road. I'm almost—

The black car flies past, Dimitri's profile clear in the back seat. I see him.

But he doesn't see me.

He doesn't hear me either as I scream for him to *stop!* Because he doesn't stop.

I scrape my hands on the low brick wall separating us. I tear my skirts climbing over. As I tumble to the gravel road on the other side, the back of Dimitri's vehicle disappears around the bend.

I'm hit with shock and not just from my fall.

This wasn't supposed to happen. I was supposed to get to the road before he passed. He was supposed to see me. I was supposed to stop him from leaving, he would confess that he'd been a fool, like in all great love stories.

You silly romantic, Alena, you naïve dreamer. Life isn't like your novels.

That's it, then. He's really gone.

This thin thread of hope that I've clung to snaps. Dimitri—the Dimitri I love—won't find a way to fight out of the rubble of his anger and come back to me. He gave up. He's gone.

It's over.

It's really over.

I collapse to my hands and knees as my body overflows with repressed anguish and painful regret, spilling out as tears into the dirt. How can a heart hold this much pain and still keep beating?

Chapter Sixty - Five

Alena

Three months later…

I still think of Dimitri every day. The sharp pain of his loss has dulled to a throbbing ache. Hopefully over time it will dull further. Perhaps dull enough so that one day, I can go without thinking about him. I still miss the old Dimitri, the one I used to know. But I no longer cling to my naïve hopes of our two souls finding our way back to each other.

Worthington Manor is all closed up. Dimitri hasn't been back since that day I saw him drive away. I wonder if he has gone back to America. I wonder if he's happy. I hope so.

Emily, Edgar, and I have moved into a larger two-bedroom cottage in the village nearby. I still share a room with Emily but at least the space is bigger. She has begun working at the local café.

Edgar has stopped drinking. He's trying to put together a business deal with an old friend who contacted him out of the blue. We have a strange, amiable relationship now but no sex.

I am finally taking responsibility for myself. I don't earn much through my administration job but I'm putting money aside. My goal is to save up enough money to convince my husband to let me out of my contract. I know a hundred thousand pounds is a lot, but I'm hoping he'll take less. Besides, I must have a goal to keep me getting up every morning.

This evening, I am at home alone. Emily is working and Edgar is meeting up with this old contact of his. I get a knock on my door. It must be Richard. He's the only one who stops in here for me.

I fling open the door without checking through the peephole. I blink rapidly when I see it is not Richard on my doorstep.

"Javier!" Dimitri's right-hand man smiles at me from my doorstep. He's wearing a dark brown suit, his hair longer than the last time I saw him. I look past him, my heart skipping a beat. But there's no Dimitri to be found. I clear my throat and smile. "What are you doing here?"

"It's good to see you again." He looks past me. "May I come in?"

I step aside for him. He enters the tiny living room. It's not even the size of my old bedroom, and barely a quarter as grand, but *I* pay rent for it so my chin remains lifted. "It's not as nice as what you're used to living in, but…"

Javier turns on his heel towards me, no judgement on his face. "Trust me, what I am used to…this would be considered a palace."

My curiosity fusses inside me. Why is he here? I study Javier, standing there with his hands folded behind his back, a twinkle in his eye. I'm not sure whether I should be scared or hopeful. Did…Dimitri send him?

"You're wondering why I'm here," he says.

I nod. "I thought you had left England," I say, hoping for a hint at where Dimitri might be living now.

"I did. I've been in America. I'm just back for a few days on business."

Of course, they're living back in America. The only reason Dimitri came to England was to ruin me, and he did that.

I let out a nervous laugh. "What business does Dimitri still have with me?"

Javier gives me a sad look. "I'm afraid I've come here of my own volition. He…doesn't know that I'm here."

Javier doesn't even dare to say his name in front of me, as if it might cause me to have a breakdown. Well, I won't have anything of the sort. "Oh. Right." I sniff. Why would I care whether Dimitri sent him or not?

"Before I give you the good news, I first need to beg your forgiveness."

"My forgiveness? For what?"

"When we were packing up the manor, I…I found your study. And your manuscript."

My cheeks burn. I had only remembered my writings after I left the mansion. I couldn't bear the idea of turning back and begging Dimitri for them. He would only use it as a way to hurt me, probably tearing the pages to shreds or burning them in front of me.

"Did you come to return it?" I frown. He doesn't have my manuscript with him. Just a small envelope I hadn't noticed he was holding before.

"Something... hopefully even better." He hands me the envelope.

It has my name on the front. "What's this?" I open it and take out the single sheet of paper inside.

"I thought your manuscript was...inspired. I took the liberty of ..." The rest of his words go fuzzy as I read over the first line of the letter.

Dear Alena,

We happily offer you a publishing contract for your book, *Beautiful Revenge*.

The rest of the letter turns into a pool of white and black. My mouth goes dry. My heart hammers in my ears. This is not possible.

I look up to Javier. He has a broad expectant smile on his face. Could he be so cruel as to manufacture a joke like this?

I am almost terrified to ask. "Is this...real?"

"Very real."

"I can't... You..." Words fail me. I do the only thing I can. I throw myself into his arms.

He laughs even as I nearly squeeze the life out of him. "You deserve it, Alena."

I pull back from him and wipe under my eyes. "Oh, Javier, you are the most wonderful man. I can't believe you would do this for me."

He shuffles uncomfortably. There's a sliver of guilt in his eyes. Some whole truth not told.

"Or did Dimitri...?" My voice cracks a little at his name.

"He doesn't know," Javier says. "I did this behind his back."

I sag a little. That's why Javier looked guilty. He is hiding this from Dimitri. "Are his businesses going well? No, I don't care about that. Is he okay? I mean, is he still angry? Is he…happy?"

Javier tilts his head. "He has found…a kind of peace."

I nod, sadness welling up inside me. Dimitri was the first person I ever told about my dream to be a writer. He was the first person I ever let read my writing and the first to encourage me. I wish more than anything that he could be the first person I told. He would understand just how much this means to me.

I brush off this sadness. I can't dwell on the past. I'm going to be published. I am going to be a writer!

Tears of happiness rim my eyes again and I press the offer letter to my chest. "Thank you, Javier, from the bottom and the top and all the widths of my heart, thank you."

He grins. "You're welcome. But you haven't read the best bit."

"What bit?" I snatch the paper from my chest and hold it out so I can read it again.

Javier laughs. "The bit about your advance."

My eyes scan the page, then find it…that magical number…

Holy shit.

A week later, my publishing contract is signed. Now I hold two very important pieces of paper in my hands. Tonight, Emily is out with a friend she's made from work. I'm home alone with Edgar. I knock on his bedroom door and enter when he calls for me to come in.

He's sitting at his cramped desk shoved in the corner of his tiny bedroom. "Oh, Alena," he says when he sees it's me. His eyes are twinkling with more life than I've seen in them for months. "I have such news to tell you."

"Of course, Edgar, but me first."

I hand him the divorce papers I had drawn up and he lowers his reading glasses onto his nose. "You and I have never been in love," I start to say what I spent hours preparing. "I think we owe it to each other to find someone who can make us happy."

Edgar lowers the divorce papers and opens his mouth.

"Please let me finish," I say, before he can interrupt. "I know that I haven't fulfilled the terms of my marriage contract. I'm offering to buy you out." I take a deep breath and hand over the second piece of paper—a check for the amount he paid for me.

A hundred thousand pounds.

His mouth drops open. "Alena… how…?"

"It's the exact amount of my publishing advance," I say quietly. I still have my job in administration, this cottage is cheap, and I can support Emily and me until the royalties come in. Besides, this is just the beginning. For the first time in a long time I have more ideas for future books than I have in a long time.

He blinks at me. "I can't take your money."

Oh God. He won't let me out of my contract. "But, I—"

He holds up a hand, cutting me off. "I won't take your money. But I will sign the divorce papers."

My mouth pops open and shut as I struggle for words. "W-why?"

Edgar smiles. "It's what I was going to tell you. I just agreed to a deal with an old business partner. I'm back in business, baby."

I smile, then laugh, because sometimes life is magical. Sometimes wishes can be bought with the light of the stars. And dreams become more than mist and smoke.

We hug. "Congratulations, Edgar."

"And to you too."

I pull back. For a moment we stand awkwardly in front of each other, two ex-partners, amicably split. If only all relationships could end this well. I think about how things ended with Dimitri and me and my heart lets out a mewl.

"I was never a good husband," Edgar says quietly.

"No, you weren't," I say truthfully, but with no malice to my voice. "But it's not too late to be a good father."

He nods.

He places the papers on the desk and signs at the bottom with a flourish. Then he hands them to me. "Happy divorce day, my dear."

I clutch them in my trembling hands. "Thank you," I whisper.

I am finally free.

Chapter Sixty - Six

Alena

One month later…

The last time I was in London was when I first arrived in England from Russia. The city seemed so grey and dirty then, stains and black moss oozing down blocky stone buildings. As I gaze out the window of the car that my publisher sent for me, I wonder if it is at all the same city, vibrant and busy with shops and people clustering the busy "high streets" of each area. I don't even mind the traffic. It gives me time to admire the gorgeous old buildings with elaborate stonework that pierce the skyline with domes and spires.

Emily is with me. We're staying at the Fifty-Four, a boutique hotel set in an Edwardian townhouse in South Kensington, a ten-minute walk from my publisher's offices. It's also walking distance to Hyde Park, the Science Museum and the Natural History Museum. In between work, I have plans to explore all these places with Emily.

I leave Emily at the hotel and walk to my publisher's office on Cromwell Street, where I'm due to meet my editor to go over the notes she's given me for my first novel—*my first novel!*

The sun gleams down through the shady green trees along the wide sidewalks, passing the rows of grand white stucco buildings, imposing pillars guarding the steps to their doors. I spot three Mercedes and one Ferrari on this block alone. I slow down near where I think the office is and glance down at the address in my hand for confirmation that I'm here, when I bump into a hard chest.

I glance up, apologies on the tip of my tongue. I freeze and swallow all words at the man standing before me, his own eyes wide with surprise.

"Dimitri." His name falls from my lips like a prayer.

Never in a million years did I expect to see him here.

He looks incredible. Same shock of wild dark hair, same strong chiselled jaw, same cobalt eyes that pierce straight into my soul. But there's something different about him. Something I can't put my finger on.

"Alena." His voice, as deep and soothing as always, rumbles through my body.

"What are you—?" we both say together.

"How are you?" we say again. A nervous laugh trills from me.

He smiles. "Ladies first, please."

I pause for a second, just staring at him. Is he…being pleasant? But…he hates me. I left him. Even after I said that

I wouldn't.

It's only when he raises an eyebrow at me that I realise he's waiting for me to speak. "I'm here to meet with my editor," I blurt out.

He nods. "Your upcoming book, of course. Congratulations."

His smile seems so genuine that I can't help but to be surprised. He knows about my book. Javier must have told him.

"And are you well?" He pauses, then asks, "Emily? Edgar?"

"We're all well, thank you." I want to tell him that Emily has moved on since their breakup. There's a man at the café where she works whom she's been seeing—not the love of her life, but a nice enough man. I want to tell him that I'm divorced now. And that I still think of him.

But I don't. I can't seem to speak.

We stand there staring at each other, people sliding around us grumbling that we're taking up half of the path, but neither of us seems to notice or care.

I find my voice. "And you? How are you?"

"Good, thank you." There's a slight glimmer in his eyes, as if he's pleased that I asked. As if he's pleased that I care.

I want to know everything about him, where is he living, what is he doing, how has he been these last four months, does he think of me, does he miss me, but I settle for this appropriate question. "What are you doing here in London?"

"I...I live here. Sometimes, that is, when I'm not in the States for business."

"Oh, I see."

"My office is close by here. That's why I'm in the area," he says quickly, as if he wants me to know he has a legitimate reason for running into me in front of my publisher's office. He runs his hand through his hair, something he does when he's nervous.

He's nervous. Could it mean…? Could he still…?

"You must know the area," I say, confidence surging through me. "I'm staying at the Fifty-Four hotel nearby. Do you have recommendations for places to eat, perhaps?" I'm being obvious, I know, asking him for his food recommendations in order to give him an opening to ask me to dinner. I can't help it. He's being so nervous and adorable and kind. Not at all like he was when I left him at Worthington Manor. He is almost like the old Dimitri. I can't help but let hope stretch her cramped wings again.

"I…" Something like pain flashes in his eyes. He tears them away from me. "I'm sorry, I'd love to keep talking but I just…I'm late. Excuse me. Congratulations again." He brushes past me and sparks shower through my body, making me gasp and sway in my ankle boots. I have to squeeze my eyes shut for a second to compose myself.

When I turn, he's walking away fast through the crowd. *Wait, I don't know how to reach you. I don't know where you live.* I'm about to go after him when I realise what's so different about him.

He doesn't look angry. There's not a glimpse of darkness in his eyes. No more rage. No more anger. *He's over me*, I realise, and my heart sinks into my toes.

Chapter Sixty - Seven

Javier

"She's here and you saw her and you said nothing?" I yell at Dimitri. I can't help it. I've been watching him for months now trying to pretend he doesn't still love her.

We're both standing in his office in South Kensington. It's taken him two days—*two fucking days*—to tell me he ran into her. He's wasting time. She might be gone already. God, he didn't even ask how long she'd be in London.

The only sign of Dimitri feeling anything is a slight press of his lips. "Calm down, Javier. We ran into each other on the street. That was it. She's fine. I'm fine. End of story."

I want to strangle the man with his own damn tie. This time last year I had to fight to reign him in, to control his emotions. In business, just like in life, he was always the risk-taker, the crazy one, the emotional one who ran at opportunities with the fury of a bull, sometimes based on nothing more than his gut feeling that something was a good investment. It almost always paid off, too. Now I'm lucky to get him to raise his voice at me. The man is completely devoid of emotions. He's become like a pale version of who he was. Who he *is*.

I know it's because he still loves her. He still hurts over losing her. Twice. Both times he now blames himself for. It's like all that anger he used to throw out to the world, he now directs inward. And shutting off his feelings is the only way he can survive the regret.

"But she's single now." I let out an exasperated cry. "And if she still loves you—"

"She doesn't. She can't love me, not after what I did to her," he says, his voice seeping with bitterness. "She's better off without me. Just let her move on with her life, Javier. I've done enough damage."

"But if she knew that you were the one to donate the money to the school so they could afford to hire her. If she knew you pulled your connections to get her husband back into business. If she knew you were the one—"

"That's enough, Javier. I know what I did."

"If she only just knew—"

"She won't know. And you've promised me on your life you wouldn't tell her."

I press my lips together. An idea flickers in my head.

Yes, I promised I wouldn't tell *Alena*, but…

"Emily Worthington." I give the girl behind the desk at the Fifty-Four Boutique Hotel my most disarming smile. Dimitri hadn't mentioned that Alena was staying here. I put in a call to her publisher, who I happen to know, and asked him where she was staying. It didn't take much for him to give me the name of the hotel. Thankfully she is still in London. "She should be staying here with Alena Worthington. Or perhaps she goes by Alena Ivanova again."

The girl shakes her head. "I'm sorry, sir. But we can't give out details of our customers."

"I don't need details, I just need you to call her room and let her know that someone is here to see her."

The girl holds up a *hold one minute* finger as she answers a ringing phone. I let out a huff and look around the reception area as I lean against the marble counter. The hotel is in a converted Edwardian townhouse. Reception is in the old foyer, slim wood floors and white walls. The stairs behind me creak as footsteps pad down them.

"Javier?"

I spin around.

And grin. I did always say I am the luckiest man alive. Emily Worthington, the very woman I am after, is standing on the bottom step staring back at me.

"What are you doing here?" she says, her youthful face all smiles and rosy cheeks. She looks absolutely stunning in a knee-length royal blue dress, black leather jacket and black ankle boots. She's become a real woman in the last few months.

"Emily Worthington," I say. "I am here to ask for your help. Can we talk?"

Chapter Sixty - Eight

Alena

It's wrong. It's wrong and I don't know how to fix it.

I scrunch up yet another piece of paper and throw it towards the hotel room bin. I let out a huff as it bounces off the rim and lands along with the other half a dozen signs of my failure.

My editor told me that my novel was perfect. *Except* for the ending. "It's just…unbelievable," she had said.

I told her I would submit a new draft ending by the time I leave London, which is…in two days and four hours. Shit. I stare down at the empty lined page. Come on, inspiration…

Nothing.

I hear the door to the room open and then footsteps. I

felt bad that Emily was just sitting around this hotel room waiting on me, so I sent her out with my new credit card, telling her to buy something lovely for herself. She must have forgotten something.

"Alena." Her voice nears.

Can't talk. Trying not to die a failure.

"Alena," she says, more insistently.

"What is it, Em, I have to—"

Emily swings my swivel chair around to face her. Her cheeks are flushed and her eyes are sparkling with light. "Alena, you have to listen to me."

I'm so curious at what could inspire such awe in her, I just nod.

She begins to talk. She spins a tale, a wondrous tale about how Dimitri donated enough money to the school so they could hire me, about how he secretly financed Edgar's latest venture which is promising to catapult him into greater riches than before, about how he bankrolled the nursing scholarship that Emily had recently gotten, and finally, about how Dimitri instructed Javier to shop my manuscript around, swearing him to secrecy over his involvement.

She finishes talking. I can do nothing but blink at her.

I hadn't even told her that I ran into Dimitri.

Why is she saying all these things?

"How do you...?"

"Javier told me. He came here and caught me downstairs as I was on my way out." A small blush played at her cheeks. "Alena, do you know what this means?"

I shake my head, my brain still trying to catch up.

"He still loves you. Desperately. He did all of that *for you*."

I blanch. "But you..."

"I never loved Dimitri," she says, quickly. "Not really. I just wanted to have someone who would love me and never leave me."

I clasp her hand. "Emily, I love you and will never leave you."

"I know that, now. But you also love him."

"No, I—"

"Don't lie to me, Leni. You suck at it."

All this time I thought he was moving on. All this time I thought he wasn't thinking of me. Dimitri did all that for me, even though he thought I would never know. I feel like laughing. I feel like crying.

She nudges my arm. "Go to him. Tell him the truth."

"What truth?"

Emily gives me a look. "Really, Leni? You need me to figure that out?"

It rises to the surface of my murky mass of emotions.

I love him. No matter what he's done.

Because of what he's done. I love him.

I wring my hands. "Even if I did want to go talk to him, I don't know where he…" I trail off as Emily pushes a piece of paper in my hands. A piece of paper with an address on it.

Chapter Sixty - Nine

Dimitri

Two days since I ran into Alena. Two days and I can still feel her bumping against my chest. I can still smell her scent.

She looked so beautiful, like always. But there had been something different about her.

I hadn't known she was here in London. I had been shocked, but recovered quickly, making sure to remain calm, pleasant, to show her that I had no lingering hatred for her. Our conversation had been going well.

Then she had asked me for a dinner recommendation. I wasn't so foolish to not understand what that meant. She wanted me to ask her to dinner. For a moment, my heart had leapt with joy. Then I realised what was different about her.

She looked free. She looked genuinely happy. *Without me.*

The realisation stabbed me deep in my solar plexus, taking away all of my breath. I knew she was better off without me but there…there was proof. Suddenly it hurt to be near her. I'm not sure what excuse I made—if I made any—before I scrambled away.

A knock on the door to my bedroom breaks through my thoughts. I shift in my chair.

"Come in, Javier," I call.

The door opens and a figure too small to be Javier walks in.

"Alena," I choke on her name. I leap to my feet, brushing my shirt down and running my hands through my hair.

She is as lovely as the day I first laid eyes on her. Not poverty, nor sickness, nor hatred of me could ever diminish her beauty. She's let her hair go wild and natural again, like I always loved. Her eyes sparkle like the sun off the sea.

"I hope you don't mind. Javier let me in." She takes a step towards me and I swear I can feel the air pressurise against my skin.

You could never be an intrusion. "Not at all," I say, trying to keep my voice casual. Unsurprised. As if The One That Got Away strolling into my bedroom was an everyday occurrence. "Please, take a seat. I can call for tea or something stronger if you like?"

I might need something stronger.

Shit. I should have kicked her out, not invited her for a drink. I wasn't sure I could stop from falling deeper in love with her. My love was already hopeless.

She ignores my offer for a chair or a drink. "I wanted to talk to you about my manuscript." Her eyes are on me, openness in them, gratitude…

I notice the pages in her hand.

Her manuscript.

That look in her eyes.

"You know," I say, my voice growing hard.

"Javier didn't tell me," she says quickly.

"Then how—?"

"It doesn't matter. What matters is why *you* didn't tell me?"

I stiffen. That's why she's here. "I didn't blackmail anyone into taking it. I just had Javier show it to publishers. They loved it. It's a great manuscript, Alena."

"You…you read it?"

I give her a single curt nod. Because I'm too busy trying not to fall further in love with her to speak properly.

"Well, thank you. Except there *is* something wrong with it."

"Wrong? No, I read it all and—"

"The ending." She steps closer. "The ending is all wrong."

"Oh?" I can't help myself, I inch closer to her. She has always been the flame that I will be eternally drawn to. She is my northern star. My way home.

"Yes," she takes another step towards me and another. "I don't think they should go to America."

"No?" I mirror her movements, my heart hammering louder the closer we get.

"I think, that's what they *thought* they wanted. But they've both made mistakes. They've both been silly and stubborn. And…and afraid of saying what they really feel. I think they want to stay here, to live here in England together, happy and in love. With Emily." We're almost toe to toe now.

"You mean Emma," I correct her, because the girl in the novel is named Emma. I think I'm correcting her. I'm falling into her eyes, losing myself in her again.

"Here," she pushes the papers into my hands, "you should read my new ending. You should read how...how it *should* end. How...I want it to end."

This is a new ending. I don't need the papers to tell me. I can see it right in her eyes. I can see all the love and forgiveness right there. It has always been there, I had just been too blind to see. I would not be blind anymore.

I set the papers aside. Alena lets out a small cry of displeasure until I take her hands, cutting her off.

"I love you, Alena," I confess. "I'll never stop loving you. I'd given up all hope that you would ever love me back. But by the grace of God, you're here. You're here, which means there's a chance that..." I swallow the knot of emotion in my throat. "Do you think...? Could you see it in your heart to one day, maybe...forgive me?"

She laughs even as her eyes rim with tears. "You silly, silly man." She flings her arms around my neck and presses her lips to mine.

I stagger under her weight for a second before I right myself and fold my arms around her, crushing her to me. Her lips are the sweetest things in the world. Like cherries. Sweeter than cherries. And the moans she makes when my tongue licks against hers, I could live on them alone. And her heart, beating against mine, is the only song I will ever need to hear.

"I love you, Dimitri," she murmurs against my mouth.

I feel like flying. I feel like I'm falling. I feel like running through the streets screaming, *She loves me!*

"You love me? You forgive me?" I ask, unable to believe my ears. "Even after all that I did."

"Of course." She smiles against my mouth and I can't help but smile too. She is the only sunshine I need. "After all, that's what love is."

This time, when I remove her clothes one by one, I do it slowly, reverently, with humble, shaking fingers. This time, when I lay her down on the mattress, I do it to worship her. To show her with my body all the things I feel that no words exist to say. Not in Russian. Not in English.

And when I sink into her beautiful body, her open, vulnerable body, I know…

I am home.

Chapter Seventy

Alena

Six months later…

"Honestly, Dimi," I say, as my world remains in darkness behind a silky blindfold. "I don't know what all this secrecy is about."

His hands are on my shoulders leading me… somewhere. It all started about six hours ago when we drove up to a private airfield and he walked me onto a plane—*his*, apparently. He blindfolded me for the duration of the flight, which honestly wasn't that bad because, well, it was the *only* thing I was wearing for most of it.

After he dressed me and we landed, he led me into a car and we drove here, wherever *here* was. All the while, he refused to tell me where we were and where we were going.

"We're almost there," he says in my ear.

I sigh, letting myself take comfort in his warmth. Wherever we are, it's a tad colder than England in autumn.

"Stay here." Then I lose his warmth.

I hear him unlock a door and then hear it swing open. His fingers thread through mine and he pulls me forward, my steps sure despite my lack of vision because I know he won't let me fall. The place we've just stepped into is wonderfully warm. I let out a small sigh.

"Are you ready?" his voice moves around me until he's behind me. I feel his hands on my hair.

Finally.

He pulls that blindfold off. I blink as my eyes adjust to the light. The room comes into view, a cosy studio apartment that's been done up; I can still smell the fresh paint. It takes me a second to recognise it.

Oh my God.

I glance out the window to confirm it and see the familiar street below. We're standing in our old apartment. In St Petersburg. He's redone it to look *exactly* like what we always dreamed it would be—the large fireplace, the desk, the bookcases, the walls painted my favourite shade of yellow.

My hands fly to my mouth. "Dimi, what did you do?"

He chuckles into my ear, his arms sliding around my waist. "You like it?"

"You *bought* this apartment?"

"I bought the whole building," he admits. "It's the first thing I did when I got enough money together."

My mouth drops open. "Most men collect baseball cards. You, you collect buildings."

"I told you I was going somewhere."

My heart lets out a guilty thud. "Dimi," my voice softens.

He squeezes my waist. "Just messing with you, lamb." He walks over to an old gramophone and turns it on. I already know what song it's going to be.

My heart soars when "Stormy Weather" begins to play. Dimitri has a wicked look on his face when he spins to me, holding out a hand. I take it and melt into his arms. And we dance.

I cannot be any happier.

"Do you remember what happened in this apartment?"

I laugh as he spins me out. "Of course I do."

I stop spinning and face him, but he doesn't spin me back in. In fact, he's stopped moving. Before I can ask what's wrong, he drops to his knees before me. "Alena…"

My free hand flies to my mouth.

"I asked you," he says, his voice trembling, "all those years ago to marry me. But I asked for the wrong reasons. I asked you because I wanted to keep you, to possess you. This time I am asking you to be my partner. My equal." He opens a black box, a huge diamond ring sitting in the centre. "This time I have a ring. Alena…" his face shines with so much love, mirroring my own, "marry me."

"Oh, Dimi," I sob. "Yes, with all the beats of my heart."

And we kiss like it's the first time.

And we kiss like it might be the last.

And he picks me up and carries me to the bed where he strips me naked, then places my new ring on my finger. We make love. And we fuck like we hate each other. Then we make love again.

Afterwards I lie against his naked body, our limbs tangled together.

Dimitri hums against my forehead. "You screamed so

loud I think the neighbours might complain."

I bury my face in his neck, my cheeks warming. "Oh God." I was *so* loud. "If they complain, I might die of shame."

He shrugs. "If they complain, I'll just get new neighbours."

I laugh. Then gasp. "You can't kick them out just because—"

"Joking, lamb."

I settle back into his arms and let out a happy little sigh. Now, I think, I cannot get any happier.

Epilogue

Alena

One year later…

I sit at my desk, working on a new novel. This one is entirely fictional, I'm glad to say. *Beautiful Revenge* released a few months ago to strong sales and my publisher is waiting for my next manuscript. I've kept my pen name as Alena Ivanova. But my real name is now Mrs Alena Wolf.

Dimitri's presence warms my side, his hand stroking my hair. His other hand rests on the desk, rubbing that old fingerprint ink stain. He rescued my old desk from Worthington Manor before he sold the house back to Edgar for a very reasonable price. Edgar couldn't stay mad at Dimitri when Emily spilled to him that Dimitri had helped make him rich again. Thankfully, he's stopped doing business with Terrance.

"Hey lamb," he says.

I smile up at him. "If I'm the lamb, what are you going to call the little one when he comes?" I rub my huge round belly.

"Or she." He leans over and places a hand on my hand on our child growing inside of me.

I laugh. "Or she. What will you call her?"

"Little lamb."

I snort.

We live in London now in a four-bedroom apartment facing Hyde Park. It's close to Dimitri's office, my publisher and not too far from the university where Emily is finishing her nursing degree. She stays with us for the semester and returns to Worthington Manor to see her father during her holidays.

"Do you think I have time to cuddle my lamb…naked?" Dimitri hums against my ear, his hand slipping over my bump and lower, making me shiver.

"Leni!" Emily's voice calls out, the front door slamming behind her.

Dimitri groans. "That girl has impeccable timing." But there's fondness in his tone. He's grown to love her like a sister as much as I do.

I shoot a *later* grin towards Dimi.

Emily bursts into my study room, which also doubles as a library with bookshelves against every single wall, comfortable couches and armchairs about the place. She's chattering away, but even as she speaks there's an anxiousness in her tone. Her smile doesn't quite reach her eyes.

Before I can ask her what's wrong, a familiar male figure walks in behind her, startling me.

"Javier," I say with surprise. "I didn't realise you were coming around."

Dimitri frowns. "Neither did I."

"Sorry to bother you both on the weekend," Javier says. He seems nervous, too. He keeps shifting his weight and fidgeting with his shirt.

Dimitri's frown deepens as he glances between Javier and Emily, now standing side by side in front of us. "Why are you here?"

"Um, so," Emily starts, "there's something that we, that is to say, Javier and I, need to tell you…"

There's a heavy pause.

"Well, go on," Dimitri says, his voice growing hard.

Emily glances over to Javier. He nods to her and she turns back to us. "I know this will probably come as a shock to you. It came as a shock to us too. What I mean to say is, we didn't mean for it to happen it just—"

"Emily, honey," I say, "spit it out."

"Javier and I are in love," tumbles out of her mouth.

There's a moment's pause.

I look over to Dimitri. He's already looking at me.

We both burst out laughing.

Poor Emily and Javier just stand there looking at each other. "W-What's so funny?" Emily asks.

I wipe the tears from my eyes. "You sweet girl. You looked so scared."

"And you, Javier," Dimitri says with a chuckle, "you looked like you were going to piss yourself."

"What?" Emily is still staring at us both.

"They knew," Javier says, the light flicking on visibly behind his eyes.

"*What?*"

Javier glares at Dimitri and me. "You knew and you didn't tell us? You let us agonize over telling you for weeks?"

"When it was so funny to let you both squirm?" Dimitri says.

"To watch you both tiptoe around when you thought you were being so discreet and clever?" I add.

"You're not...mad?" Javier asks.

Dimitri and I protest all at once.

"Emily is like a sister to me," I say, "if anyone deserves her, it's you."

"And Javier, it's about time someone made you a happy man," Dimitri says.

Javier and Emily look at each other. Emily gives him a shy look and reaches for his hand. "Now we don't have to hide it anymore." She turns to us and grins. "I guess you won't mind if we announce that...we're engaged!"

I let out a small scream and Emily joins in. I fling myself at her, wrapping my arms around her neck. *This* is how I should feel when my very best friend gets engaged. This time she's getting engaged to the right man.

Dimitri and Javier clasp hands. "Congrats, mate. Looks like I'm breaking out the good scotch tonight."

Once I tear myself away from Emily, I congratulate Javier with a hug too.

We break open a champagne bottle and that bottle of scotch, soda water for me. The four of us sit close and talk and laugh.

I let out a squeal suddenly, almost spilling my drink into Dimitri's lap.

"What's wrong?" Dimi says, his hand on me instantly.

I'm too damn excited to speak. I grab his hand and place it on my belly. The baby kicks again. This time it's Dimitri who yelps. He leaps from his seat and begins to jump around the room like a lunatic. "We'll put a cot here and a rocking chair beside it so you can rock our little lamb to sleep. Oh, and here…!" As Dimitri paints our future with his hands, Emily and Javier crowd around me, their twin hands on my belly. I catch the tiny look between them and I know that my little lamb may get a best friend soon enough.

Music blasts from the gramophone we brought back from St Petersburg. Dimitri has turned on a rocking swing number. He runs over to us and has the three of us up and moving and laughing in seconds.

As he swings me in his arms, the sound of Emily's giggles in my ear as Javier dips her, I think, now—*now*—I can't get any happier.

This is how to make a home. You take a house and, no matter what the furniture looks like, you fill the rooms with laughter and love.

The End

Mr. Blackwell's Bride

A Good Wife Novel
Sienna Blake

Drake
This marriage was supposed to be another business deal. My latest investment, a means to an end… I need an heir. Which means I want her belly swollen with my child before the year is out.

She was supposed to be my perfect little bride. Quiet. Uncomplicated. Unemotional.

I didn't foresee the stunning firecracker who tumbled into my life and woke things in me I thought were long dead. I didn't count on her turning my world upside down.

And I definitely didn't plan on falling for this beauty.

Noriko

This marriage was supposed to be my sacrifice. A way to save my father, a means to an end… I need to remain childless. So I can exit the contract at the end of the year.

He was supposed to be a boring old man. Distant. Uncomplicated. Passionless.

I didn't foresee the rude, arrogant, beautiful brute who makes my body react like fire and embers. I didn't count on there being more underneath his gruff exterior.

And I'm definitely not supposed to fall in love with the beast.

Even though this book is part of a series, it is a standalone novel.

Coming 12 November 2017

Love Sprung From Hate
Dark Romeo 1
Sienna Blake

I didn't know she was a detective, the only daughter of the Chief of Police.
I didn't know he was a mafia Prince, heir to the Tyrell's bloody empire.

It was only supposed to be one night.
God help me, I can't stop thinking about that night.

So when she walked into the interrogation room, my heart almost stopped.
I can't believe he might have tortured and killed someone.

I have to avoid her at all costs.
I will be his downfall.

So begins a deadly game of cat and mouse, of blood and lust, of love and duty, and of an attraction so fierce the consequences are inevitable...

Inspired by Shakespeare's Romeo and Juliet, this is a retelling for mature audiences. Don't enter the Underworld if you're scared of the dark.

Out now
Read on for an excerpt of Love Sprung From Hate

"Follow" Me on Amazon
to get an alert when Beautiful Revenge is live.
http://bit.ly/SiennaBlake

Or sign up for my Newsletter
for new release, sales & giveaways alerts, plus a free ecopy of my full-length romantic thriller, Paper Dolls:
www.subscribepage.com/SiennaBlake

Join my Dark Angels group
For exclusive giveaways, get a sneak peek into what's coming up next, vote on covers and blurbs, and interact with me personally.
http://bit.ly/SiennasDarkAngels

Did you enjoy Beautiful Revenge?
The best way you can show me some love is by posting a review at your retailer! Don't tell me, tell the world what you think. (Then message me so I can thank you personally.) It really helps other readers to decide whether my books are for them. And the number of reviews I get is really important. Thank you!

If you're a Blogger,
please signup to my VIP Bloggers List for ARC opportunity alerts:
http://bit.ly/SiennaVIPBloggers
Blogs will be verified.

Stay sexy,
Sienna
xoxo

Stalk me! I like it

www.siennablake.com
www.facebook.com/SiennaBlakeAuthor
www.instagram.com/SiennaBlakeAuthor

Books by Sienna Blake

Bound Duet
Bound by Lies (#1)
Bound Forever (#2)

Paper Dolls

Dark Romeo Trilogy
Love Sprung From Hate (#1)
The Scent of Roses (#2)
Hanging in the Stars (#3)

Beautiful Revenge
Mr. Blackwell's Bride ~ *out 12 November*

Excerpt of Love Sprung From Hate

Roman

There she was.

Julianna. Leaning against the bar on the other side of the room. For a moment, I wondered if I had dreamed her out of thin air.

Sweet mother of God, she looked incredible. The sight of her hit me like a fist in my gut. The music seemed to go funny in my ears. The body that her outfit earlier only hinted at was now on display: taut legs in a black dress that clung to her curves and fell several inches above her knee. Her hair was loose and fell in soft waves over her shoulders, down the sides of her breasts.

She was stunning. More stunning than I'd imagined her, and trust me, I'd imagined her in all sorts of ways all evening. I stepped out of the VIP section, ignoring my friends calling out for me. I pushed my way through the crowd. It seemed like every motherfucker wanted to get between her and me.

She broke eye contact with me and turned to the guy who had sidled up to her, trying to speak to her. My blood simmered. Now he was touching her, playing with the ends of her hair close to her breasts. Too fucking close to her breasts. He grabbed her wrist, yanking her closer to him. Instant fury like a torrent of fire rose in me. Nobody fucking touched her. Nobody hurt her. She was *mine*.

"Get your fucking hands off her," I yelled, rage booming though my voice, startling the club-goers around me, not that I gave a shit. I shoved the people in my way aside. I would kill the fucking son of a bitch who dared lay a hand on her.

Julianna twisted her arm, rolling it aside so that the asshole was forced to let go. She stabbed her heel into his toe causing him to hop before he tilted off balance. She shoved him down over the bar, pinning him by twisting his arm around his back. He let out a yelp.

Holy. Shit.

I skidded to a halt beside them, my anger turning to red-hot lust. I had never seen a woman handle herself like that before. I could do nothing but stare open-mouthed and mute at this powerful, gorgeous creature, respect building in my gut.

"Don't you dare touch me again, asshole," she said to him, her voice hard and fierce. The sound of her cursing made my dick harden.

Julianna looked up to me as the guy she had in an armlock made whining noises against the bar. She gave me a smile like nothing was the matter. Unbelievable.

"Oh. Hi," she said, almost shyly. "Again."

I gave her my best charming grin. "I was just coming over to save you…"

She raised an eyebrow. That tiny movement was a challenge. "Why?" she said sweetly. She applied the slightest pressure to the unfortunate guy's wrist and he let out a low pained cry. She jutted her chin out and a defiance flared in her feline eyes. "Because I'm a *girl* and all I need is a big strong man to come save me?"

"No, because you're a human being. I don't like it when I see other human beings being treated without respect. Not when I can do something about it."

She shifted, seemingly surprised by my honest comment, embarrassed even. "Well…I don't need saving."

"I can see that." I indicated her unfortunate victim. I spotted a bouncer heading towards us. I held my hand up to signal to him that I had it under control. He nodded and kept his distance. The bouncer was a low-level street thug who'd been trying to climb my family's ranks for years. Part of the reason why I could score the VIP treatment here at the last minute.

Julianna spotted this exchange. "Do you own this place or something?" she asked.

I shrugged. "I know some of the guys who work here." Here and pretty much every hot spot of Verona. I didn't want to explain to her how I knew them. Tonight, I wasn't Roman Tyrell. Tonight, I was just a guy and she was a girl…

"Can you let go of me now?" the man whose face was squashed up against the bar interrupted in a whining tone.

I shot Julianna a grin and leaned in close to him. "Tell the lady, you're sorry and *maybe* she'll let you go."

The man's eyes widened when he saw me, recognition flaring in his eyes. "Y-y-you."

That's right, stupid fucker. You just pissed off a Tyrell. "Tell her you're sorry," I repeated.

"I'm sorry," he cried out.

I stared up at Julianna and was struck again by how stunning she was. She raised an eyebrow at me as if she knew what I was thinking. I gave her one of my trademark half-smirks. "Are you satisfied with his apology, milady?"

"Only if you *don't* try and touch up a girl without her permission again," she said to him.

The idiot was silent.

I leaned in closer and growled. "When the lady speaks to you, you answer her."

He let out a whine. "Okay, okay. I'll never do it again."

Julianna applied some more pressure to the guy's arm and he let out a louder cry. She was staring at me, a half angry, half lustful look in her dark eyes. "Tell Roman," she said, her voice coming out low and heated, "that I don't need him to fight my battles for me."

"What?" the guy cried.

"Tell Julianna," I said, matching her stare, "that she should learn that it's okay for a man to help her. It doesn't make her weak."

"Tell Roman, that he's an arrogant ass who has no idea what it's like to be a woman in a man's world."

"Tell Julianna, that I can't tell if she wants to fight me or fuck me tonight."

Julianna's red lips pulled up into a smirk. "Why can't it be both?"

Jesus, fuck. I felt my cock surge with blood and I swallowed back a groan. I wasn't finished. "Tell Julianna that she's the most stunning creature I have ever seen."

"What the fuck?" the guy stuttered against the bar.

"Ever?" Julianna asked, an amused eyebrow raised.

"Ever." And I fucking meant it. She was captivating. Intoxicating. A lioness among sheep. This wasn't a woman who'd fall at my feet and gaze adoringly up at me. She'd demand to stand beside me. She'd demand to be pleased. She'd deserve to be pleased.

I had to have her. Here. Now. Anywhere. I'd take her here on the fucking bar if she'd let me.

I nodded down at the single annoying thing standing between her and me; the asshole she'd thoroughly put in his place. "Maybe you should let him go. Before you break something. We both know it's really me you want to get your hands on."

Julianna snatched her hands off him. He stumbled back off the bar, rubbing his shoulder and his wrist.

"Get out of here," she told him, her eyes still pinned on me.

"You two are fucked up," he muttered before he hurried into the crowd.

We both eased closer as if out of instinct, our eyes eating each other up. My cock was hard as a stone, painful against my jeans, and I didn't give a shit who noticed.

"You're very sure of yourself," she said.

"Doesn't mean I'm not right." I took the final step towards her, filling up the space between us. In heels, she came up to my eye-line. I could smell her perfume of pears and musk, an intoxicating combination. Sweet yet fierce. Like she was.

"Do you think we made our point?" she asked. "To him, I mean.

"I think you put the fear of God into him."

"Are you kidding? I just disarmed him. He was pissing his pants when he saw your face up close."

"Well," I folded my arms, knowing that it showed off my biceps. Look at me, like a fucking peacock preening myself in front of her. "I am pretty scary."

She smirked and copied my stance, folding her arms over her chest, making her breasts push in and up. Jesus, I could fall into those fucking breasts.

Eyes up, Roman. She's a fucking lady. It took all my willpower not to follow those curves down farther. I tore my eyes away and looked up. Even under the dim light, I could see her cheeks were flushed.

"Maybe you're scary to *some* people," she said, her voice low and teasing.

I grinned. The lioness wasn't scared of me. Interesting. I leaned in closer like I was about to tell her a secret. "Maybe, I should scare you."

She stepped right up to me and lifted her chin as if to make a point. "If you want me to run away in fear, you're going to have to do a better job than that."

I lowered my face so close we were breathing in the same air. She had peppermint on her breath, and I noticed the gold flecks in her amber-coloured eyes before they dilated into large black holes I was falling into. Everything about her was drawing me in, closer, closer. "Maybe, I want to watch you run."

"Maybe, I want you to chase me."

Purchase now to continue reading

Acknowledgements

I was so worried that Dimitri was too cruel and hateful. Big massive epic thanks to Kathy of Book Detailing. Without your encouragement, this novel might not have seen the light of day.

Thank you to my early readers & reviewers: Sammy of Just Let Me Read, Julia of The Romance Rebels, Shabby & Laura of Book Bistro Blog, Wendy of Girls Just Wanna Have Books, Maria of Devilishly Dirty Book Blog, Patricia of The Bookery Review.

To Terrie of Just Let Me Read. Thank you for running the show while I focus on my writing.

Thank you Romacdesigns for that beautiful cover, as always.

And thanks to Christie of Proof Positive for your eagle eye.

About Sienna

Sienna Blake is a storyteller & inksinger, wordspinner of love stories with grit, and alter ego of a *USA Today* Bestselling Author.

She loves all things that make her heart race—rollercoasters, thrillers and rowdy unrestrained sex. She likes to explore the darker side of human nature in her writing.

If she told you who she really was, she'd have to kill you. Because of her passion for crime and forensics, she'd totally get away with your murder. *wink*

Printed in Poland
by Amazon Fulfillment
Poland Sp. z o.o., Wrocław